Short Stories, Songs, Music and Lyrics

by

Precious Jesus Christ in Heaven
with Harry W. Doren on Earth

DORRANCE
PUBLISHING CO
EST. 1920
PITTSBURGH, PENNSYLVANIA 15238

Dorrance Publishing Co
585 Alpha Drive
Pittsburgh, PA 15238
Visit our website at *www.dorrancebookstore.com*

ISBN: 978-1-6470-2462-8
eISBN: 978-1-6470-2900-5

Harry W. Doren Critique of His Short Story Book

Jesus Christ has written the greatest short story book ever.

I know as I read this greatest short story book tears run down my face like falling rain. It holds me with such overwhelming intensity as I read it over and over again. The title of the precious book is *Short Stories, Songs, Music & Lyrics By Precious Jesus Christ in Heaven With Harry W. Doren on Earth*. It is so gripping so intense that it's almost impossible to stop reading. When you read it you know instantly it was written by Jesus his great mind, thoughts, feelings and masterpiece was conveyed to me Harry W. Doren as Jesus moved my pen displaying his great thoughts on each beautiful story in the book. I read it over and over again it appears to be even greater more magnificent each previous time it is read. I know it is well above my caliber of thoughts, writing and greatness it had to be from the immaculate Jesus Christ that is why the title states it. I feel that it will be the very best of all top seller books ever written. It is truly a masterpiece by precious Jesus Christ.

CONGRESSIONAL MEDAL OF HONOR

Just a medal on a uniform, a civilian might not recognize it,

Yet that is the highest military award given to an American soldier.

The Congressional Medal of Honor is the nation's greatest tribute for gallantry under fire.

Of the millions of men and women who have served their country,

From the bloody Civil War to the jungles of Vietnam,

The Medal of Honor has been awarded to only an elite few, less than four thousand,

Many of whom are dead or maimed.

Anyone from generals to privates, from Army, Navy, Marine, or Air Force,

From all parts of this beautiful land,

May be awarded this symbol of gallantry and heroism,

Which has no comparison in our society.

These great Americans have earned their nation's highest esteem.

The president may award the Medal of Honor in the name of Congress

To a person who, while a member of the Armed Forces, distinguishes himself by gallantry,

At the risk of his own life, above and beyond the call of duty.

The medal is powerful yet simple in appearance

With a five-point star suspended from a blue-silk ribbon containing thirteen white stars,

Which represent the original states.

What separates the recipient's valor and bravery from that of his fellow soldiers?

What drives or sparks him to so much heroism?

Is it fear for his own life or the lives of his companions?

Or for freedom or a love for his free and beautiful America?

To qualify for the medal, the soldier's heroic act must be verified by at least two eyewitnesses.

It must be so outstanding that it clearly distinguishes above and beyond the call of duty

From lesser forms of bravery and at the risk of his own life.

Here are a few of the extreme acts of heroism by the cherished holders of the Medal of Honor:

In a platoon, several men were wounded. An enemy grenade landed in the midst of them. A PFC grabbed the grenade and pulled it to his chest as it went off, giving his life to save the lives of his comrades.

Another Medal of Honor recipient killed six snipers armed with automatic weapons. His ammunition gone and being mortally wounded, he killed two more enemy soldiers in fierce hand-to-hand combat, his actions saving the lives of many members of his platoon.

Still another recipient, severely wounded by enemy snipers, charging across an open area,

And braving enemy fire for a second time, but wounded again, unable to walk,

He crawled fifteen meters to the cover of a rock, continually throwing hand grenades

To destroy a machine gun nest.

As he threw his final grenade, which destroyed the enemy position,

He was mortally wounded.

President Theodore Roosevelt wanted the Congressional Medal of Honor badly.

President Harry Truman often told men as he presented it, "I'd rather have that medal than be President of the United States."

And General George Patton once said, "I'd give my immortal soul for it."

Generals salute the men who wear the Medal of Honor.

From an extremely grateful nation, we give our endless thanks and everlasting respect to our Finest fighting soldiers, only a tiny few who excel with so much heroism

Have reached this highest plateau.

The loyal recipients of the Congressional Medal of Honor.

Baseball

(Man)

Baseball is the finest, most-loved sport in all the world. It is America's greatest pastime. Everyone, from little leaguers to college-age to the coveted major leaguers, it is loved by all, from intense no-hitters in pitching or the unbelievable plays in the infield to the miraculous catches in the outfield. Then the overwhelming, breathtaking homeruns and watching the favorite teams roaring and screaming in victory and yelling and cussing in defeat. They watch in cold, rainy, and sunshiny days. The baseball players are paid millions for their outstanding abilities. Little kids to grown-ups adore the beloved game of baseball played by such greats as Ruth, Gehrig, Mays, DiMaggio, Williams, J. Robison, Mantle, and Trout cheer on and on. Such superstars and hundreds of others, too many to mention, so deeply loved by all their fans and family for a lifetime of our beloved baseball to be played and watched by one and all, day after day, year after year.

You're the Reason

(Man)

You're the reason I love—love and exist. You are my everything, my precious true love. You are guilty of inserting all your special memories in my mind where they are locked forever. You are the reason I smile, laugh, and cry because you are my world. You're the reason I awake each morning so happy you are in my loving arms with hugs and kisses. I could never find a love like yours because you are the reason my life is so extremely exciting now. I can't think of anything but you day and night. You are the reason I am the luckiest man in all the world.

(Man/Woman) Because our love is maxed out every moment of each day, how could we be so special to receive a love so super as ours? We are the reason our love is so unbelievably great, and we only hope and pray it lasts forever and ever.

My New and Endless Love

(Man)

I cried a tear for you my dear. You just gave me a sneer. So I had myself a beer to drown my tears, and I began to fear because you were so near but were leaving here. It was oh so clear I could no more love you, dear. I will wander aimless with no more cheer. So it is crystal clear, I must find me another dear, so there will be no more sneer, so my new dear will come here and we will have a lifetime of cheer. No more fear, just me and her, forever dear.

We Are All the Same in God's Eyes

(Woman)

All the races, creeds, and colors are the same. It doesn't make any difference if we are black, white, brown, or red. We are all God's people. All the races, creeds, and colors went to war to fight and defend this great America. Some died, others live to battle for freedom for this beloved America. Yet we still fight among the colors that God made us all, loved us all. That is the way it should be, must be. We are all Americans, children of God's Great Kingdom. We all work together, love together, and live together. We must love, be good, be kind to each other no matter what race, color, or creed we are. That is what God wants, and that is also what is necessary to reach the Kingdom of Heaven. We're all loved and meant to be in the great and beautiful heaven in the wonderful hereafter with our great savior, Jesus Christ.

I Have A Lifetime

(Woman)

I have a lifetime of greatness you have bestowed upon me. I have a lifetime of smiles, grins, and happiness we have had together. What a wonderful lifetime we have had, and I have a lifetime of all the great and wonderful, very special things we have done for each other. Each day we live, we walk, we talk and smile at each other—what a special, wonderful life we have together. We wake up in the morning thinking of each other, smiling and so happy as we go to work, our minds wandering back to each other. What a very special life we have together. We come home oh so happy to see each other and have a great evening together. Then we go to bed and dream of each other. What a supreme lifetime of happiness we are having together. We could not wish for a greater, more special lifetime together and hope and pray it continues in the great hereafter.

In a Cabin On a Cliff
in the Rockies

(Man)

In a cabin on a cliff in the Rockies stood my love.

(Woman) I said, "You come for me by tomorrow or I am jumping off this cliff. I love you so very much, but I will wait no more. The overwhelming torture to my heart and mind will not let me continue to live without you.

(Man) I was injured by a grizzly bear attack. My arm and leg were clawed, but I survived. My love for my darling is so very strong. My arm and leg are not quite healed. I must man-up, and even though I still have pain in my arm and leg, I can't let my beloved darling leap off that giant cliff, so I will climb the huge mountain to rescue my one true love in a cabin on a cliff in the Rockies, who has been waiting for me oh so long. I know I can make it before she leaps off that cliff because, if I don't, I will have to leap also because I could never stand the pain and agony of losing my darling. I will climb that terrible mountain even injured, then (Man/Woman) we will be in love even more, the two love birds in a cabin on a cliff in the Rockies.

This Or That

(Man)

I wake in the morning. Is this the right time, or is that the right time? So much this. So much that. I don't know what to do. Should I do this, or should I do that? I get confused. If I do this, maybe I should have done that. I walk down this street, but should I have walked down that street? I am driving down this road, but something says it must be that road. I turn around on this road to go down that road. I look at this beautiful girl. Is she the right one for me, or is that girl for me? She smiles at me, and my heart does a flip. I know it's not her. That one, I know it's her. She is so beautiful, kind, and considerate. We fall in love almost instantly, so there is no more this and no more that, just her and me in a beautiful world of happiness.

Will It Be Yes,
or Will It Be No?

(Man)

Oh, will it be yes, or will it be no, when I ask those beautiful words to her? I tremble and shake for the answer she may utter to me. I must take the chance for her to be with me for the rest of my life. Would it be yes, or would it be no?

If she says yes it will be like heaven on earth, but if she says no, it will be like the cold dark down under. I must get the strength I need somehow, somewhere to ask that precious question. Will it be yes, or will it be no?

I fall on one knee and ask, "Will you be my wife, my precious sweetheart?" Will she say yes, or will she say no?

I feel a tightness engulf my mind and body. Then you speak those beautiful words, "Yes, my darling. I love you," and it is the happiest day in all our life. What a super wonderful life we will have together now and forever.

The Gentle Giant

(Man)

I saw The Gentle Giant so far away on the mountaintop I was climbing. He has done so many, many outstanding deeds and rescues on the mountainside, in forests, and in rushing rivers. He has saved so many children, women, and men from all types of danger, misfortune, and disaster. He is known and respected by all the people in that village, and most of them he saved from all types of terrible pain and agony.

There is a monument of The Gentle Giant in the village of his huge and muscular body, depicting all the many wonderful glories he has performed, that Gentle Giant we love, need, and cherish so very much, every day of our lives, to protect, guide, and defend us from all the severe problems we may encounter.

The Glory of God

(Woman)

We must always be good for the glory of God and treat Him with reverence, kindness, and the greatest respect, for He made us and put us on earth to serve Him, to love and cherish His greatness. You see all the beauty in the world, the blue sky, the tall mountains, and green valleys. They are works of our King and Savior, precious Jesus, our God on high. He is our leader, our healer, and our overwhelming love. We must walk the straight and narrow, so we can sometime live in His precious Kingdom up above, for there is no greater glory than to live with the wonderful Jesus. So whatever you do, be good, kind, and love and help all the people, for those are the words of our beloved Jesus to enter his great Heaven.

Miss Everything

(Man)

I want to tell you how much I love you, but when I see you, I get all tongue-tied and cannot speak because I see you, so pretty, my mouth flies open with great amazement at your outstanding beauty. My eyes are locked on you and cannot move. You have me spellbound in a trance, a precious trance that is unbreakable, with only overwhelming love. I have never seen a lady so outstanding in so many ways. Let's count the ways: You are outstanding, beautiful, kind, loving, and with great smarts. Oh, what a lucky man I would be if I could date, love, and marry you, where we would share everlasting happiness and an abundance of love!

Christmas Tree

(Woman)

Pretty little Christmas tree, hiding in the snowy woods from me, I know what you look like because I dreamed of you last night. Oh, how pretty you looked all perfectly shaped with a gorgeous green color! I have never before seen or noticed such a sweet pine smell as that coming from you. You are just the right height. What a wonderful Christmas tree all decorated with pretty colored lights and bulbs. You will truly be a special sight for all of us to enjoy. Now I see you peeking out of that brilliant snow-capped mountain for me to take and enjoy with family and friends for a precious Christmas.

Are You Ready?

(Man)

Are you ready to tell me you love me or not? Are you ready to talk to me, smile at me, or pass me by? I am ready to take a chance on you. So I say hi and you say hi back. I ask if you are ready to talk and walk with me, and you say yes. I am ready to go on a date with you, are you ready? And we go to lunch together. We have so much fun. She smiles and laughs.

She said she was ready to like me because we have so much fun together. It looks like we are ready to fall in love because we both are really crazy about each other. The next step was we are both ready to marry and have a wonderful life with each other for years and years and a wonderful family together.

Don't Rain On My Parade

(Man)

Don't rain on my parade. I saw you, I love you, and you, I hope, will be mine before it rains on my parade. You are one of a special kind, so very special, so please don't rain on my parade. So please date me, kiss me, and love me before there is rain on my parade. You look so beautiful, talk so sweet, so please come with me before there is rain on my parade. I want to marry you, love you, live with you always because I could never find a lady as outstanding as you. So come with me, and don't rain on my parade. Let's have a lifetime of love and happiness, now and forever, so there will never be any rain on our parade.

Our Loving Life

(Man)

I had a glimpse of your beauty as you strolled by my house. I could not believe how pretty you stood out. I don't think I have ever seen such a lovely girl as you. I wanted to say hi, but bashfulness stepped in, and I let you slip away. I pray to God you will come back to my lonely home again. I must overcome my shyness and talk to you. Then I saw you down the street. I told you my name, and you told me yours. We began to talk, and to my great surprise, we dated.

I fell in love with her almost instantly and she with me. What a beautiful life. We have a girl and boy, the spitting image of my beloved wife, and what a wonderful time we have in store. Each day our love grows stronger, sweeter, and more sincere. I can only hope we have so many precious, loving years together before our time on earth is ended.

Just Because of You

(Woman)

Just because of you I have my happiness. I have my love, my darling, my sweetheart, which is all because of you. I awake in the morning, and all day and night I think of only you. It is just because of you I think each day of kissing, hugging, and loving you. Just because of you, you make my heart, my mind, my love jump and blast out of control. Just because of beautiful you. I would have no happiness, no contentment, no love without you, precious darling, but I thank the man above and so many down on earth because, just because of you, I have a world of endless happiness. I could never wish for more because, just because of you, I have it all.

Missing

(Man)

He cried his eyes out on that cold winter night when she left him. He knew he could never find another love to come close to the precious love he had for her. He searched here and there for his beloved, darling wife. She was all the world to him. His life, his heart was shattered and broken. He informed the police she was missing. He could not sleep, eat, or imagine what happened to his precious sweetheart who was so pure, so sweet, and lovely. They got along so extremely well.

The phone rang. "If you want your wife back, it will cost you a million dollars, or she is dead."

He called the police. It seemed like hours grow into days as it dragged on. In a few long days, the police called and said, "We have your wife safe and the dirty dogs that took her."

So we will once again have our pure, immaculate love for now and forever.

Trapped

(Man)

You have me wound in a knot. I can't breathe. I can't move. I try to talk, but no words come out of my mouth. Is it because you have me trapped with love in all my body by your overwhelming beauty? You have a beauty I have never seen in all my life. I try to move my arms, my lips, with no results. I am paralyzed in an unbreakable lock of love. If only you would notice me, maybe smile, talk, or wave, and I could end this beauty hold in which I am frozen. Then I see a little glance, and my arms begin to move. You smile and my body is released from the frozen lovelock in which you had me. I see, I feel, I move in our most precious loving life of pure, unending love.

Rain

(Woman)

The tap-tap, ta-bing as the rain hits the old tin roof on my little cabin in Ohio—it makes me so content, so happy and sincere. It almost puts me in an unbelievable trance. I look out the window to see the rain watering the flowers, grass, trees, and crops. It is so peaceful to listen to the tap-tap-tapping of the rain hitting on the old tin roof of my little cabin in Ohio. It makes me so happy that life and living is so great, so great to be alive in this great land and wonderful world of ours. The rain relaxes and makes our life so precious. It also is lifegiving water for all of us to drink. The water makes the grass and all the crops on various farms grow and other foods we eat to survive. It's a wonderful miracle we truly need for food, water to drink, for cleaning, and much more we need for survival. Without rain, we would truly perish.

I Am Dreaming of You

(Man)

My dream is of you. I don't know who you are or where you are, but I will find you some day. I may need God's help. I know you are beautiful, sweet, and sincere because I dream of you every night. I know you are so special, kind, and considerate. We will meet some day soon. I pray to God we will be together forever in a world of endless love. I have searched high and low for beautiful you. I know you exist because I dream of you always, and then the precious miracle happened, and I saw you appear in the distance. My heart beat profoundly as you came closer. You seemed to sense we were being united by a spiritual meeting, controlled by the great one up above.

We at once fell in love for a lifetime of happiness to be. It was a miracle sent from God, or it surely appeared to be.

You Flee and She's Back to Me

(Man)

Turn me loose. What's the use? Set me free. Let me be. I don't want any more of the. I work so hard for us to be, but I can see you want to flee away from me. It's so sad to let you flee, and there's no glee for me. So I will wander over yonder looking for another she once again, so we will be happy, she and me, in a lifetime of endless glee. So everyone can see it's truly a life to be. It's so clear and sincere for us to be loving, and that is what it's all about. So I can shout, our love is stout, so we will take a nappy because we are so happy and live a life of snappy happy.

Dreaming

(Woman)

I am dreaming every day and night of you, and I can only hope and pray that brings you back and my dreams come true, and I am dreaming you will return to me some day. I am dreaming you will walk through those doors and give me the greatest happiness, although I know you have left me for another. I thought I had died and truly felt like it when you said our marriage had ended, but I still have faith through my dreams I can persuade you to come back to me, darling.

When I first met you, I knew you were the one and only, so I will dream of you always and everywhere for your return and know I must have failed you somehow, somewhere. I can only keep on dreaming, so my many dreams will meet your dreams, and you will come back to me, sweetheart, where there is no dream, just everlasting truth that you come back to me, and we love each other now and always.

In a Second of Time

(Man)

I saw her in a second of time, but it took a lifetime of love to keep, to hold, and cherish her. I know in that second of time, that very precious second of time I first saw her, she was the one, the one and only love for her and me forever. It seemed as though my heart stopped beating and started beating as one, hers and mine, in that precious second of time.

(Woman) We seemed to love, breathe, and think as one in those seconds of time to years of our loving life. We were transformed together in an endless lovelock, which will last us forever into the great hereafter thanks to those precious seconds of time.

(Man/Woman) Two loving people could not be happier, more content, or more in love as it transpired in those few seconds of time. It was a miracle engineered by Heaven. We couldn't believe such a life was possible, but now we are living proof it truly happened in those few seconds of time because years and years of our super wonderful, glorious love has proved it. Our love started in those beloved seconds of time.

Where Did I Go Wrong

(Man)

Where did I go wrong and fail her so much? Had you known what pain and agony that you were in, wouldn't you have treated your darling wife like a saint instead of just so-so? She was your world, your life, your everything. How could you have dropped the ball so far down? You should have known the way she treated you was that of a king and you treated her to just a so-so life. I know if you get a second chance, you would surely treat her like an angel as she truly deserved because she was so sweet, so wonderful, that everyone cherished, as you should have also because you now know a woman so precious, sweet, and wonderful is one of a very special kind that comes around once in a long, long lifetime. So now you know you should have loved her so very, very specially and kindly, so she would never leave you, just love and adore you, but you may never get that second chance again to show her all your love. But if you ever do, I am sure you will treat her as an angel sent from God's great Heaven.

You Were the Love of My Life

(Man)

You were the love of my life—how could I have been so stupid, so dumb to let you slip away. I will do whatever is humanly possible to entice you back to me. I know it may well be the most difficult endeavor I have ever encountered.

I will move heaven and earth 'til I win her back into my loving arms. I will buy her flowers and gifts to help persuade her to return to a love of which she has never seen or dreamed. It must be so outstanding that she could never refuse. I will show her love, kindness, and sweetness until I know she could never refuse my unending love and respect.

The Weather Around My Little House in Ohio

(Woman)

The weather is so wonderful surrounding my little house in Ohio. The wind blows free through the big trees in my front yard. When the rain comes down, it makes a tap-tap here and a tap-tap there on the tiny roof of my little house in Ohio. Sometimes sleet forms like falling ice with a bang-bang here and a bang-bang everywhere on my little house's tin roof in Ohio.

When the weather turns cold, the snow filters down like tiny balls of cotton on the roof, the yard, the trees, the bushes, like a beautiful white blanket covering everything in sight. Later in spring, the sun appears and heats everywhere, and the snow melts. Pretty flowers blossom, and green leaves appear around my little house.

It is so sweet, so wonderful. It makes me so happy and joyful to be alive in my little house in Ohio, and I am so thankful to be there and enjoy it all.

Not "She" or "Her," Just You, Darling

(Man)

I want to be with you, not somebody else, just you, darling. I want you, not her. Just you to walk and talk to, not that girl, just my girl. It's not her, it's my darling you, so I must work hard to keep you, not her, just my beautiful you. She doesn't spin my world out of control, just you and you only, my precious sweetie. I am in so, so much love with you, my pretty lady, not her. All the love and kindness you give me and make me the happiest man in all the world, not her. Just you, my very special darling with whom I have fallen madly in love and want to keep to love and to cherish you forever.

Love of Thelma

(Man)

I heard someone was looking for me to create trouble. I was not sure whom it was, but I had to find out, so I entered the bar. The noise was extreme. Everyone was yelling as I walked through the door and saw some big bruiser charging at me at high speed. As he came close, I hit him with a left hook and a right. He fell slightly and leaped to his feet with even more violence spurting from his nasty mouth. I didn't even know the reason for his anger at me. I had never seen him before.

Before he charged at me again, he said, "You took my wife, Thelma, the love of my life. I am so sad and so lonesome. You have destroyed my life, John Bates."

Just as he swung and missed, I said, "Stop. Check my driver's license. My name is Ed Jones."

He looked with tears in his eyes, at my name and said, "I'm sorry. I thought it was you. I must keep searching for the dirty dog that took my wife, Thelma, because my life has ended without my precious wife, Thelma, who is my everything."

Can You Imagine

(Man)

Can you imagine just how much I love you, my precious darling? Can you imagine what a beautiful love the two of us could have, to have and to hold, to love and to cherish for a lifetime? I think we both can imagine what a superior love would explode when the two of us kiss, hug, and love each other. I know you can imagine what a world of love we have in store. When the two of us get together, people turn around and look with overwhelming awe when they look and imagine the very, very special love in which we are locked and frozen, sweet and wonderful. It seems such a precious and real love, must ask and not imagine if that sexy, smart, beautiful, darling will be my wife.

So I ask that great and wonderful question of my sweetheart, and just as we both imagined, she said, "Yes, my darling." Now our love will be the greatest for a wonderful lifetime and not imagined but really real and true, now and forever.

Left Me

(Man)

I thought I saw you in my precious dream last night, or was it just a misprint in my memory bank? You looked so beautiful, sexy, and sincere, the same way when you left me in that terrible, fatal car crash on that snowy, icy road in Montana. I never married again because our love and marriage was so immaculate I could never find a match that would even come close to our precious love. So I just hold the precious memories of our everlasting love in my memory bank to draw on each and every day of my life, so everlasting and pure, until we meet again in that great hereafter, when our love will reunite and blossom for that shiny ever and ever.

To Love You Always

(Man)

If I had a lifetime to live, I could never find a girl to match your beauty, kindness, sweetness, and your sharpness. I have looked high and low, here and there, and everywhere, but no matter where I look, there is nobody to match your overwhelming greatness in any way. I will treat you like the very special lady you truly are, so I will always love and hold you as my precious angel. I love so much to love you, cherish, and adore you for now and forever to be beside you, talk to you, live and love you, now and forever, in a kingdom of endless love.

Hard Work

(Man)

I work in the fields for various crops. It is so hard, so hot, and miserable for just a few dollars a day. I wish at times I could run away and hide and not come out because the work is oh so hard. It hurts my back, my legs. I'm always in pain, day after day, with no rest in sight and just a little bit of money. Although, I must continue so I can feed, house, and support my precious family, for without my work, they would truly perish, so my work is so important to all of us surviving for a better life in older years when we can rest in peace and joy 'til death do us part.

Missing You So Much

(Woman)

The tears ran down my face like falling rain. I cried, I sobbed, but no relief. Every moment of every hour, I think of you and cannot sleep, eat, or work. You have me in your mental grip, and there is no escape. When you left me on that bitter cold winter night with that terrible terminal illness, I was defeated, alone, a woman with no cause, no hope. It has destroyed me in so many ways. There is no peace, no joy. Just torment. You have me locked with overbearing sadness in my mind and body for now and forever. The only way out is when I die. I hope and pray we will once again meet in the Great Kingdom above, and our lives will once again blossom as the greatest love.

Jesus

(Man)

We saw you in your little bed in Bethlehem. Little did we know you would be our spiritual, religious savior, the great Jesus Christ. We waited for you so long, and now you're here to guide, teach, and give us everlasting life. Oh, how lucky we are to have you to lead us through all the many paths of life, to keep us from danger and all the sins of the world. You show us through your precious teachings the right and correct way to live, so we may reach Your immortal heaven to live with You for all eternity in a place so unbelievable that none of us can imagine.

Our Precious Loving Life

(Woman)

If nothing happened when we went out last night, why do you keep looking back at me? I feel you want to go out again, so I am asking you out a precious second time. Yes, I would love to go out with you again. We had so much fun. We went out and had lots of fun, danced, and kissed. I fell in love that precious night, and it looks like you did the same. We seemed to really fall in love. We like the same things, have so much fun, and really fell deeply in love. We later married and really have a very special precious, loving life together.

The Fluffy Snow

(Woman)

The fluffy snow comes down like tiny balls of cotton, landing on my darling and my face and melting away. Oh what a beautiful white Christmas this is going to be. The beautiful white coat of snow covers the ground, trees, and buildings and looks so pretty like a fleecy white blanket, sparkling and shining. I have my precious darling by my side. We are in love, so very much. We seem to think, act, and love as one. He is the miracle of my heart and mind.

We build a fluffy snowman, which looks so funny in the snow. We laugh and have so much fun throwing snowballs at each other. I could never be separated from my loving sweetheart. We are welded together—mind, heart, and body. We watch with so much love as the pretty, fluffy snow dances to the ground in a gorgeous, covering whiteness.

Love Me or Leave Me

(Man)

Love me or leave me. I can't take one day loving, next leaving. It is way too hard on my heart, my mind, and body. I think you are going to love me, and you talk about leaving me. Don't you know my love for you is so very special? Then you turn right around and say you want to leave me. I am so confused. One time you love me, next time you are leaving me. Can't you make up your mind and tell me you love me instead of one time you love me, next time you want to leave?

We were walking down the street, and a big truck, out of control, headed straight for my darling. I grabbed her and pushed her out of the way as the screaming truck hit my foot and broke my ankle. My darling was so happy that I saved her life. She said that was the greatest thing anyone had ever done for her. "You saved my life. I love you so much! So no more loving and leaving. We will just be loving and loving, and no more leaving, ever."

Jesus is Waiting at the Doorway to Precious Heaven

(Woman)

Jesus is waiting up above in the precious doorway to immaculate Heaven. If we are good enough, He will tell us so we can walk through the precious doorway to God's great Heaven. He is standing in the doorway to precious Heaven. He will let us know if can enter the doorway to his great kingdom. If we have been good enough we will make it to the top and through the precious doorway to beloved Heaven. Oh, how I hope and pray I have been good enough to make it through the door to God's great Heaven.

Then the miracle happens. He gives his permission for me to enter His beloved Heaven. Oh so very happy I am to be with immaculate Jesus in God's great Heaven forever, and I hope and pray all others join.

I Am In a Whirl

(Man)

Stop the merry-go-round of life. I am sick to my stomach and dizzy as a bat and have no sense of humor or control because my darling has wandered away from me. I don't know where she is or why she has left, but all I know is my life is in a whirlwind, going round and round. I see no stop in sight, just whirling and whirling with endless anger and despair. Her leaving was so quiet and so silent that I didn't know for hours she had left me and our little farm in Nevada. It seems as though the horses, cows, and pigs have dropped their heads in sadness. Oh, how could I ever get her to return to me and our little farm in Nevada where there is endless sadness all around and overwhelming joy and greatness for her return?

I Need to Treat You Like an Angel

(Man)

Had I known you were coming, I would have had everything set up to please you like the greatest of love for each other. I would have really rolled out the red carpet, so now I must work ever so hard to make up the precious things I have forgotten to do for you. Now I will treat you like the very kind, sweet, and wonderful angel you truly are. I will buy you flowers, jewelry, and a large diamond ring, so I can marry you, love you, and cherish you every day of our beloved life.

Choo, Choo Train

(Woman)

I want to ride on the beautiful choo, choo train with a choo, choo here and a choo, choo there, that goes down the railroad tracks with a choo, choo here and a choo, choo there, passing through towns, cities and states with a choo, choo here and a choo, choo there. All the people onboard are so very happy, looking out the windows at all the beautiful scenery with a choo, choo here and a choo, choo there. It climbs the high mountains and roars down the valleys with a choo, choo here and a choo, choo there. It arrives at its various stops with everyone cheering, with a choo, choo here and a choo, choo there. It makes all of us so very happy and excited that we reached our destination with a choo, choo here and a choo, choo there and then starts all over again.

Our Love in Trouble

(Man)

We are so far apart. How could we ever get back together again? It seems we are in different locations. It appears we are stuck on different islands in the South Pacific. When we try to console each other, it appears to go in one ear and out the other. Why is it so hard to talk to each other when we were once so much in love? Where have we gone wrong to let a love like we once had slip away to no-man's land? We try to get together, but it seems like we are trying to climb an icy hill, going up a little bit, coming down a lot.

We were once inseparable. Our love was unbreakable. We were united as one. Then the terrible thing happened. My wife was in a car accident. I carried her to my car and took her to the hospital. She was in a coma for months, and then the beautiful miracle happened—she awoke and said to me, "Darling, what happened?"

I said, "You were in a car accident, and I took you to the hospital. You were in a coma for months."

She said, "You saved my life, darling."

She acted as if we were never in trouble. Our love was just as before, beautiful, wonderful, and loving, and we will keep it that way forever.

Jesus Our Savior

(Man)

I am Jesus, the great God in Heaven, the Christ your Lord, all good and pure. I will lift you up to Heaven if you are good, but if you are bad, down you go where no one wants to be, for Heaven is a place of endless greatness for the pure of heart and love for all others. If you have walked the walk and talked the talk in kindness and love in a lifetime of loving and helping each other, I will take you with me, cherish and hold you in My beloved kingdom. So you must do what is right, love each other, help each other, so you can come with Me forever. Be kind and do what is right, so we can be together someday in My home up above where there is nothing but the greatest love and happiness.

My Darling's and My Life

(Man)

It was a code of silence, so no one should ever know you and I are even talking with each other. You are from the rich side of town. Your mom and dad are wealthy, and mine are on the poor side of town. I like you, and I feel you must like me also, but I don't see how it could work with you and me. Your mom and dad would surely frown on us going together. I am sure they want you to be with and marry someone more financially well-to-do than me.

(Woman) She said, "I don't care. I love you."

(Man/Woman) So we began to date and fall more deeply in love. Mom and dad raised all kinds of discontent, but my darling said, (Woman) "I don't care. I love you."

(Man) So I'll ask my darling to marry me. Her parents disowned her.

(Woman) So we bought a home of our own and planned to have a wonderful, happy family together, loving each other so madly.

We are sure in time we will convince mom and dad to love us. What a beautiful life we have in store.

America Number One

(Woman)

Good morning, America. You shine so bright, day and night. America, you are loved so very much by all the people who love you, adore you, worship you, and fight to protect you. Some live, some die to protect our great America. There are always more people loving America each day, loving and cherishing this great, beautiful, God-loving America.

America is so very beautiful to love in, to work in, live in. No country can match its overwhelming greatness. We always hold it to the highest standards as we love, cherish, and protect it with our lives to make very, very sure no other country ever overtakes it. America remains undefeated and is loved and respected always as our beloved number one in every way.

Our Love in Trouble

(Man)

I want to be your irritation. I want to irritate you so you will notice me. You are so beautiful and sexy. I want to meet you, date you, and love you. If I irritate you, then you may look at me, notice me, so I bump into you, and you look at me, notice me. I must be so careful I don't make you mad when I am kidding. My love for you is so, so special, and I don't want to endanger or lose it. I think from my joshing you I gained your attention. You look at me and smile. You seem interested. We go out on dates and have a world of happiness. We hug, we smile, we kiss. It seems so real. I must ask you now if you would do me the greatest honor in all my life and marry me.

Your precious word back was (Woman), "Yes, I love you."

(Man/Woman) So we will both, I am sure, work hard to have the greatest marriage possible, children, love, and happiness, day after day, year after year.

Beloved Jesus, Please Save Us a Place in Heaven

(Woman)

Great God in Heaven, oh how I love you, sweet Jesus. You are my world, my love, my life, and my everything. You are all the world to me from a beautiful Heaven up above. Oh how You shine on me every day of my life. You are my super guidance. You show me, teach me right from wrong. You are always keeping me on the straight and narrow with Your precious teachings. If I waver or do wrong, I say a special prayer and almost instantly I am brought back from that wrong I was about to do. I owe You everything, precious, immaculate Jesus. Please save me a wonderful place in Your very special Heaven where everyone and I can join You when our time on earth has ended.

I Have the World at My Feet

(Man)

I have the world at my feet. I am kicking and gouging to make it to the top. Sometimes I gain one step, and other days I go up two or three. I must keep trying to reach the top. It is so difficult because sometimes I slip back one or two steps. I must always be in shape, exercise, and stay in shape always to be called up from the minor leagues into the coveted major leagues. I am rated about fifteenth best hitter and fielder in the minors. I have jumped several numbers. I am twenty years old and hope I get to the top five best in all minors next year.

To my surprise, the next year I was rated number two of all the great out-fielders in the minor leagues. Then the great call came to me from the Yankees. They wanted to give me a chance in the major leagues. The first year I hit 308 and 51 homeruns with 105 runs batted in. So I have now made centerfield with the great New York Yankees, a feat that is so overwhelming and unbelievable.

Long, Long Time

(Man)

It took a long, long time to find a woman, a very special woman, like you. In that long, long time I looked everywhere, here and there, high and low. You were not to be found in that very long, long time. I see you now, so cute, pretty, and beautiful. I can't believe it took such a long, long time. You are smiling at me, and I smile back in this very short, short time we met. We hit it off right away, no long, long time. We later married in a surprisingly short, short time.

What a wonderful life we have now, you and me and children. We hope it will last a long, long time. The years fly by. It seems like a short, short time, but really it was a very long, long time. My wife and I are now old. We have been together a long, long time. I can only hope and pray we will all be together for a long, long time in the great hereafter.

Won't You Be My Pain
in the "A - -"?

(Woman)

Won't you be my pain in the "A - -" and love me oh so much? You are my little pain in the "A - -," but what an outstanding lover and sweetheart most of the time. I can easily put up with that little bit of your "pain in the A - -" because I know I am a bigger "pain in the A - -" to you. We seem to ignore or dismiss being a "pain in the A - -" to each other because we are so madly in love. Sometimes we don't even realize we are such pains to each other because we turn right around and love each other so preciously time after time.

So who cares about the "pain in the A - -"? We love so much to be with each other. It's such a beautiful miracle of happiness.

A Feeling, A Very Special Feeling

(Woman)

I had a feeling for you the very first time we met, and then I saw you again, and the feeling was stronger, so I asked to meet you again, and you said yes. I looked into your beautiful blue eyes. They seemed to lock together with my eyes, and the feeling grew more intense. I had a feeling, a very special feeling you were the one, that very special one with whom to fall in love, to raise a family, live a life of everlasting love. It seemed that very special feeling was the same feeling for you. When we first touched, it seemed we were on fire with a love so very strong. It seemed to bind us together as one in a special, a very special feeling of everlasting love that won't be broken forever and ever.

Leaving Me

(Man)

I felt the breeze on my neck as you ran out the door screaming you would never return and jumped into that old 1968 Chevy pickup truck and squealed the tires, throwing dirt into the air.

She had been mad for days, but I never thought she would leave our little home. I will search high and low for my darling, who has left me in a cloud of dust and gas fumes as she bolted away, leaving me only with a two-wheeled bicycle, which I will pump up hills and down valleys 'til I find my darling and try my best to entice her to return with me and hope we have a world of endless happiness for both of us to receive.

Making Quick Stops and Long Stops

(Man)

I want to make a quick stop for you. I want to buy you some flowers to show you how much I love you. It's another day now, so I will quick-stop to buy my precious darling some candy because she has been so sweet and wonderful to me. Oh, how much I love this beautiful, wonderful darling of mine!

Today I am making a long, long stop for my one true love on her birthday. I will buy her jewelry and diamonds because she is truly worth it and so much more. I am falling head over heels and so very much more in love, and I feel that wonderful feeling. She is oh so crazy about me also. All the quick-stops and long-stops of loving her and her loving me, no man or woman could feel so much tremendous love we have shared with each other.

I am making another long, long stop, by far the most precious quick-stop or long-stop I have ever made. I am buying my beloved sweetheart a diamond ring, and I will ask her if she would do me the greatest honor ever and marry me.

To my greatest delight, her most wonderful, special words back to me were (Woman), "Yes, my darling. I love you." Then, "I love you still, I always have, I always will."

To Be a Winner

(Woman)

She fought, hit scratched to make it to the top. Nothing was easy. She had to work hard to make it, to be a success. She now knows it is so easy do something wrong and slip from the top rung of the ladder and no longer be at the top. She works hard doing things correctly to stay at the top, but some days she fails and slips from the top.

She now knows she must always be vigilant, to try and be correct most of the time to succeed and push forward to be a winner. She knows she will work hard to keep herself in a positive winning way to succeed.

My Large Piece of Heaven

(Man)

My little piece of heaven is you. You may be my little piece of heaven, but you are all the world to me. I am thankful every day, for you are my everything. I love you in all the precious ways you conduct that most beautiful life of yours. Oh, how very, very lucky I am to have, to hold, to cherish the greatest little lady a man like me could ever have. I thank every day to just be associated with a sweetheart like precious you. I have looked high and low and everywhere, but there's none to match or even to come close to my very large piece of heaven in this very beautiful, special, loving world of ours.

Our Little Cabin in the Rockies

(Woman)

In my little cabin in the Rockies I am so happy. I listen to the running water in the stream outside. The beautiful flowers are just coming up on this gorgeous spring morning. They are all pretty colors, red, green, white, blue, and many more. The awesome sun is peeking over the mountaintops where deer, antelope, and bear are feeding in the lush green grass. What a wonderful happiness this is, but I am truly sad and missing one thing. I must go to the city and find me one very special man with whom to spend the rest of my life in our little cabin in the truly gorgeous Rockies. I know he will be oh so very happy in our little cabin in the Rockies where we will live in such great happiness for eternity.

More Love and Kindness

(Woman)

Why is it so easy to do wrong when we should be doing right? We scream and yell at friends and neighbors at times but should be giving them kindness and consideration. We wake up in the morning grouchy to family members instead of being happy and friendly. We never know how much time we have here on earth, so it is truly better to always be kind, nice, and loving to each other here on earth. We never know what terrible sickness, accident, or misfortune may cause the loss of a wife, husband, child, or neighbor. It is better for your mind and body to always be nice and treat each other as we would want to be treated ourselves. What a wonderful world it would be if everyone were kind and good to each other. We would all be so much happier, content, and peaceful in this beautiful, loving America.

I Must Put On the Big Boy Pants

(Man)

It is time for me to put on my big boy pants and tell her I am sorry for the wrongs I have done to her. The big boy pants may be loose or tight, but I must find the words to ease or stop the hurt and pain I brought upon my beloved darling. She has always been kind, sweet, and smart, and now I have treated her so unkindly and snarly when I should have given her pure and lasting love. I am trying now to correct the wrong I have done to her, but it seems she wants no part of me. I try to get her back now, but she says, "I don't love you anymore because of the way you treated me before." I walked out the door forever, causing me endless sadness.

Let Me Count the Ways
I Love You, Precious Darling

(Woman)

I love you my darling, and you said, "Why do you love me?" I said let me count the ways I love you so much. Number one is because you are so kind and considerate. You are so nice to me. Number two is your beautiful hugs and kisses drive me out of my mind. Number three is you are always helping me to stay on the straight and narrow with your precious love, never to wander. Number four is the way, the very precious way you guide and help our family and me through all the pitfalls of our precious life. Number five is without your wonderful, precious love and guidance, our family and I would truly perish, but thanks to you and all your beloved help, love, and consideration, we now have the finest family possible, thanks to you, precious you, my beloved darling, unmatched by any here on earth.

Christmas

(Woman)

It is the night before Christmas, and all the boys and girls are wide-eyed and jittery, but they must go to bed early in hopes old Santa Claus will bring them that pretty, shiny present they have been dreaming about for months. They twist and turn and can hardly go to sleep in hopes Santa will really deliver tonight, so they can tear those beautiful colored papers holding their very special prized gifts they have been in search of for months. Santa Claus slips in oh so quietly and delivers those precious presents. The boys and girls jump up and find the great and wonderful presents about which they have been dreaming, and everyone is very happy as joy fills their hearts and minds.

The Most Beautiful Dream to Come True

(Man)

I had this beautiful dream my darling to be was standing on an island in the South Pacific. She was oh so beautiful, her pretty brown skin matching her gorgeous brown eyes. I felt in those very special seconds, those very special seconds of time, I was in paradise. The precious dream continued in that overwhelming moment, that very special moment in time. I saw the beautiful blue water as it washed upon the beach as my darling swam into the on-rushing water. Oh, so beautiful and sexy she was! The seashells washed all over, making the beach look ever-so-pretty. The palm trees, all loaded with coconuts and beautiful birds chirping in the trees, if this is not heaven, it must be a very, very close second.

So I awoke all smiles and oh so, so happy. I must choose that immaculate dream through which I just lived in those very special seconds that continued in those moments, those very wonderful moments of time, that I saw and fell in love with my darling, of those very special seconds and moments of time, so I headed to the airport and went to the gorgeous South Pacific islands and made it true, finding my very special, darling wife to live a life of endless happiness.

Be Careful

(Woman)

Don't settle for a loser. You must become a chooser. So look high and low, so you can obtain a douser. Although after all of that, he could become a boozer. So be real careful when you're a chooser that he's not a loser. Check everywhere, here and there, for the correct schmoozer so you don't wind up with a snoozer. Even though after you do all of that, he may be a user and take all of your money, love in a sleazy manner. So always be on alert, check it out in all the different places to get the greatest douser and both of you can have a very happy world as schmoozers.

If Only I Had a Second Chance

(Man)

I had a lifetime of love to give to you. Where did I go wrong? Did I not treat you like the angel you were? How could I have been so stupid when I had the chance to treat you like a queen? I don't know what I was thinking to have let you slip away. It doesn't make any sense what I did when I loved you so very much. Was I so far off the straight and narrow to see what was really happening? It doesn't take a genius to know I must not have been paying enough attention to you to see all the warning signs you had to have been casting out to me. How could I have been so much alone to bypass all the danger that was happening? If only I had a precious second chance, I would treat you like the very, very immaculate darling you truly are. I can only hope and pray the precious second chance will surely appear.

Oh, Where Have We Gone?

(Man)

Oh, where oh where have we gone? We have gone so, so far apart. Our love is no more. Oh, where have we gone to no man's land? We were once so much in love. We were inseparable. Now it seems we are wandering aimlessly. There is no rhyme or reason. Oh, where have we gone and our precious love we once held as gospel? We don't know if this happened, our precious loss of love, day by day or at once. Oh, where have we gone? We are still together but oh so very far apart. What has happened to our love, which we once thought was so sincere? Oh, where have we gone?

(Man/Woman) As we were walking down the street, a bolt of lightning hit a tree in front of us and knocked it down. We were in a beautiful, loving trance or daze. As we awakened so slowly, it seemed like a heavenly awakening we never encountered before. We were once madly in love like "oh, where have we gone" never happened, and we are keeping this beautiful madly in love forever encounter everlasting in our hearts and minds.

I Am Falling More
and More in Love

(Woman)

I am falling in love more and more every day, again and again. I have no control. You have my mind and heart in your mental grip, causing my mind and heart to fall in love again and again, over and over, more and more in love, yes love, with precious you. What a tremendous feeling it is, all day and night. I am falling deeper and deeper in very special love with you, my one and only very precious lover. It is a love so welded and frozen to never be broken in a lifetime, a very special lifetime, now and forever. It draws us together more and more, a feeling so overwhelming that both of us can hardly move. Just smile and enjoy a feeling so supreme neither one of us wants to lose. Just accept and let it grow and grow, now and forever.

Let the Beautiful Music Play On Forever

(Man)

Come and sing, let the beautiful music play on. Let the beautiful music enter our hearts, minds and bodies. Let it roar through trees, yards, and houses. Everyone is singing. This beautiful world is in in tune and singing and roaring. What a precious day this is. It seems everyone is singing, happy, so content, so in love. Please don't stop the music. Let it roar on and on. It appears the birds, dogs, and cats, all animals, are in tune as the beautiful music plays on. Please don't stop that music. It is so beautiful. Keep singing one and all. This music makes this the happiest day in all the world. People far and wide are singing the music. Oh so beautiful the music, oh so beautiful! It has everyone so happy and content. There is no sadness today, just happiness and love as we all sing the beautiful music as it roars, screams, and puts all of us in the happiest day in all of our lives. Everyone is so happy, so kind, so loving. So let's have this beautiful music play on forever and ever with no end in sight.

Our Lord Jesus, Our Savior

(Man)

The little baby Jesus sleeps so soundly in His tiny manger as joyous people look on. His halo shines above His small head. It glows so bright. It lights the evening and night. Everyone is cheering and smiling. We have our beloved Jesus Christ, our one and only Savior to help and guide us into eternity. He will lead and teach us throughout our years on earth, and if we listen to His word, we will one day reach the beautiful Heaven with Him. But we must be good and kind to each other and help everyone because that is God's teaching: to always do what's right, be kind, love, and help each other as He truly wishes. And when our time on earth is ended, we can enjoy all God's super love and everlasting happiness.

With a Little Help, We Can Do Anything

(Woman)

With a little help, we can do anything. We can talk, walk, smile, and love each other to the max and beyond. With a little help, we can help the ones who have strayed away from goodness and bring them back to greatness. Each day of our precious life, we can help each other with kindness, wellness, happiness, and rightness to seek out someone in a bad way or place to get them away from danger and onto safe ground spiritually or to wellness or to just plain help in so many, many ways. Just like a sick neighbor or hungry friend needs help, work, and kindness, whatever it is we can do it to help each other. We can do it to help this God-given world of ours and the beloved people within it. We can help one and all for a better, more precious people and beautiful world in which we live, love, and cherish.

I Want Your Volcano of Love for Eternity

(Woman)

Won't you be my volcano and erupt for a lifetime of endless love into my mind, heart, and body, and let it flow day and night as long as you and I are here on earth? Never let the hot burning coals smolder or burn out. Just let those red-hot burning coals of love from you and me burn hotter, wider, and longer, so we know nothing else, just that hot, burning flame, jumping higher and higher in and out of the receptacles of our minds, hearts, and bodies. No man or woman can douse the burning flames from our onrushing love, which appears to burn stronger, longer, now and forever and ever.

My Mama and Papa
Are the Greatest

(Woman)

I sit on the porch with my precious mommy who is so old now. She's so sad these days and moves so slow and all hunched over. I feel time here is getting shorter. I will surely miss my beloved mama and papa. I could not have survived without all the precious guiding, leading, and protecting me through all the pitfalls of life. I will be forever grateful for the beloved care they bestowed on me in so many ways. They are truly giants in the field of mamas and papas. They are in a league of their own, certainly one of a very, very special kind, truly first in so many fields of care, love, and superior guiding as mamas and papas.

He Is My Precious Lover

(Woman)

People say, "He's no good for you and he will be trouble for you." How do they know who is good and who is bad?

Even mom and dad said, "He may not be good to you." How do they know who is good and who is bad?

He treats me so very special and oh so good. He's so loving, kind, and considerate to me, that man standing there, so sweet and wonderful in that precious doorway to my heart. Do other people know he treats me like an angel? I feel I am the luckiest woman in all the world to have been united with a sweetheart, a lover of his unique kind, who excels as one in a precious million in this beloved world in which we live, love, and cherish, for now and forever and ever.

More Sunny Days Than Cloudy

(Woman)

Just another ugly day. Where have all the good, sunshiny days gone? Is that all we get anymore—cloudy, dreary, rainy days? Are there no more birds chirping in the trees on a sunny day? It makes us so sad on cloudy, rainy days. We want to be so happy and joyful on those precious sunshiny days where we can go outside, walk, play, and have so much fun on those sunshiny days. The children have so much fun playing outside on sunny days. It seems people's faces are all smiley on sunny days and all grump-faced on rainy, cloudy days. It is known there are more sunshiny days in the year than cloudy, rainy days, so we all will be more happy than sad in this beautiful, precious world in which we live and love.

Just One More Time

(Man)

If I had just one more time, if I had it, I would give you a million dollars just to see you again, my sweetheart. I would swim the rushing river to hear your beautiful voice or withstand the charging bull just to get a glimpse of your beautiful face. If only I could touch you, hug and kiss you again, I would be the luckiest man in all the world. I know to make love—precious, sweet, immaculate, overwhelming love—to you again would make me a king. I can keep on wishing and hoping, and I know it won't be possible. There is no way it can happen because you are now bound for heaven. My precious hope now is we will meet up above, and all these loving things will come true.

My Wife, A Lady Unseen in This World

(Man)

Please release me. Let me go. I have found another who loves me oh so much more, who treats me kindly and sweetly. No screaming, no arguing—just pure, sweet love. I can't believe the beautiful love we now have. We never fight, just kiss, hug, and make beautiful love that flips, skips, and makes my heart beat out of control. When I first saw you, oh so beautiful, sexy, kind, and wonderful, I knew you were the very, very special love about which a man can only dream, and now you are mine. What a one in a million man I must be to land a lady, a very, very special lady, whom this world has never seen. Oh how lucky, so very lucky I am to receive a lady so beautiful, so sweet and wonderful as my darling wife, a lady unseen in this world since the beginning of time.

Tick-Tock Time

(Man)

Tick-tock-tick-tock. The time flies by so fast. I am getting older, and I have so many things to do. Tick-tock. I need more time to show my wife and children all the finest happiness they deserve. Tick-tock. So I must exercise, take my vitamins, so I will be around a long time. We have places to go and wonderful things to see as the tick tock, tick-tock time flies by. We need to work hard, my family and I, to reach our precious goal, and I know we will do it before the tick-tock time on earth is finished.

Anything You Can Do, She Can Do Better

(Man)

Anything you can do, she can do better. She smiles better than me, laughs better. She's oh so much prettier than me. Anything I can do, she can do better. She dances and hugs better than me. She works, she talks, and she walks all better than me. She is in a world of her own to always excel and do better than me. I don't get mad. I just love her more because both of us are out of control in love with each other to the very max. It is very far from my thoughts that she can do anything better than me. We love each other so very, very much. Neither one of us cares she can do anything better than me.

Just Goodness, No Badness

(Woman)

You are my goodness, no badness. Just more and more of your very special goodness, kindness, sweetness and never any badness. I am so very lucky to be surrounded with your very special goodness. I must work day and night to always keep the beautiful goodness going, so no badness can enter our precious life.

He wants to do the same for me—just beautiful goodness and no badness. If we both wake up each morning and through and through the very special day and night we only share goodness with each other and shove badness completely out of our life, what a gorgeous love, life, and world we will have to live, which will rock our world in endless happiness.

How Could He Betray an Angel

(Man)

You didn't deserve what happened to you. You were always so good and kind to him. What happened to him? Why did he treat you so mean and cruelly? What is wrong with him? Doesn't he realize how great you are? You are so very special. He is nasty to you. I don't know what his problem is. It appears to me he doesn't want to change. How could he be so cruel not to love you like the great and wonderful angel you truly are.

So if he doesn't shape up, you will have to separate from him, and I am sure he will suddenly realize how very precious, sweet, wonderful, and great you truly are and come begging and pleading back to your very, very special love, seldom seen in a lifetime.

Our Love's On Fire

(Man)

Our love is on fire, it's burning higher and higher. The furious flames of our love are snapping and crackling. What a burning hot love we have. Our love torch is out of control. No matter how much water is poured on the fire, it just burns longer and stronger with a beautiful, loving flame. There's no smoke, just hot, burning fire from our wondrous love. The beautiful, hot-burning flames could not be put out by all the fire engines in the world. Our love just gets hotter and hotter as we love each other to the maximum and above. The flames from our fiery love shoot here, there, and everywhere. Everyone says, "What a hot, burning torch your love is casting."

The heat from our fiery love could heat a city on a cold winter's night. The only way our furious flame could go out is when our time on earth has ended, and we just leave smoldering ashes. Then the flame of our love will burst out again, higher and higher in the great hereafter.

What a Precious World This Would Be

(Woman)

What a precious world this would be, no more shooting or killing each other. Instead, we would give love and kindness to each other, the young, the old, the sick—more love and kindness—never killing, never mean or nasty things to each other, just that beautiful love and kindness for each other. Oh, just look at all the smiling, happy people in this big, wide, beautiful world of ours! Never before had we seen people helping young, old, and sick. It has happened. The most precious beautiful miracle has taken place. The cars are honking in kindness to each other, everyone waving and helping each other. What a most wonderful, beautiful world this would be, could be, must be, for all of us to reach our maximum happiness and our greatest chance to make it up above where there is eternal love and happiness that runs forever and ever.

I Need You So Much

(Woman)

I need you. You need me to climb that tall mountain of life. We need each other to succeed in our wonderful world of love. We will need each other's great advice to succeed in our wonderful world. It is so much easier to have both of our hearts and minds to solve every day's precious problems. You are so smart, kind, and wonderful. I would truly be lost without your super smarts and understanding. I would be lost in so many ways without your outstanding knowledge and insight to help us through all the pitfalls we will encounter throughout all of our precious life together.

Come Back to Me, Trinet

(Man)

Come back to me, Trinet. You are my life, my love, my very existence. It's crystal clear the huge love I have for you does not get cloudy. It remains so clear. So come back to me, Trinet. You are the one, the only one that bursts my heart with endless love and happiness. Where have you gone, my beloved Trinet?

I never knew a person could ever hold so much sadness, so come back to me, Trinet. Have you left me just for a short span or a long, long time? I miss you immensely because you broke my heart and destroyed our love, so come back to me, Trinet. The agony in my heart can only be cured by your loving return. I hope wherever you are, the loss of your love will drive you back to me, and our love will reunite once again, stronger and purer, so come back to me, Trinet.

Then the precious miracle happened. She was standing right there, all pretty and sexy in the precious doorway to my heart, and she uttered the words, "I am oh so sorry, my beloved darling. I missed you so very much. I will never leave you again, just love and cherish you forever and ever."

And I said to my precious sweetheart, "I missed you so very much. We will never part again. You are all world to me and have come back to me, Trinet. I loved you then. I love you still. I always have. I always will."

I Have An Angel

(Man)

I have an angel, a very special angel, sent from God's great heaven. I knew she was an angel with the halo around her pretty head. Then she spoke, and the words seemed to float, words kind and sweet, out of her beautiful mouth. My mouth flew open, and I was in a trance, so magnificent were her looks, her words. I was in a beautiful love-holding grip. I knew at once she was the one, the one and only love for me.

She said to me, "I am here because I know you are the love for me."

My heart stopped beating. How was it possible for an angel such as she to fall in love with a man like me?

So I asked my precious angel, "Would you please do me the greatest honor of my life and marry me?"

She answered in the most beloved words, (woman) "It would be my greatest love to marry you, my darling."

What a precious, wonderful life we both will have to cherish and hold each other in endless love.

My Beloved Mama and Papa

(Man)

I give you my beloved mama and papa, everlasting love and the finest of respect. You have been the greatest mama and papa a son could ever have. You have given me a world of love and understanding. When I have been in the dumps, you have brightened me up right away with your special love and kindness. Oh, how could I ever repay all the kindness, love, and knowledge you bestowed upon me! How lucky a son I have been to have the finest mama and papa for which a son could ever wish or dream of having.

You have helped and guided me through life as the greatest masters of being a mama and papa this world has ever had. You are truly one of a kind, in a league of your own. Through all the years of perfect teaching, you guided me through all the ups and downs of life's many problems and enjoyments. You have guided me religiously to be a good, kind, loving, and helpful person to others, with schooling and knowledge to work every day. My wife and I will thank you always for your unending, precious help, and we will try our very best to do what your love has taught us—to raise our loving children as you so perfectly raised me—but I feel I could never reach your perfections, but I will continue your precious teaching.

My Precious Wife

(Man)

You were always the smart one, the kind one, and considerate one. That is just one of so many reasons everyone loves you, respects you for all you have done for all of us. We would be in a world of trouble without you, without your great kindness, sweetness, and brilliant understanding. You are without a doubt the finest, sexiest, most wonderful wife a husband could ever have, on whom I rely every moment of every day. I would truly be lost and beaten without your precious knowledge and love. For sure, I am the luckiest husband in this beautiful world to be married to the most outstanding lady in all the world.

Our Precious Lady for a Lifetime

(Man)

To have and to hold from this time forward. She said yes. I couldn't believe it. My world, my life has changed 180 degrees. I was unsure… not certain and at times in doubt. Since I met my precious lady, I am a new man, confident. I am more in love with that very special lady who is very seldom seen in a long, long lifetime. She clicks, excels in so many ways. I can't believe she's so outstanding in every way of her special life. Since we met and fell in love, to have and to hold, from this time forward, for the rest of our treasured life.

Our Precious Jesus
Endless Thanks

(Woman)

I see you, precious Jesus, every day and night in this miraculous mind and body you have given me. Oh how overwhelming is my thanks and appreciation for you, beloved Jesus, to give me life, happiness, and thanks for putting me here on earth in this great America. Every day and night, I thank you for my beautiful husband and children with which you have blessed me. My happiness, my health, my family, my friends you have given me, precious Jesus, our great Lord and Savior, God in Heaven. I see all the poor people, sick, hungry, injured, and the sadness in the world and pray to You that You will help them one and all, they may have the same wonderful greatness You have given me, so they may have all the great health, happiness, and love You have bestowed on me. Thanks, my beloved savior Jesus Christ, now and forever.

We Will Meet Again Up Above

(Man)

She is waiting at the gateway to heaven where I will meet my darling sometime when my life here on earth has ended. We will meet and love as before, only more in the beautiful kingdom up above. She had to go first, my darling. I feel she was needed up above, because she was so great and wonderful, to help everyone. She was so outstanding here on earth, always helping others. I am sure she was noticed by her greatness down here, so that is why she was chosen so early to help in heaven. It will be so great, so wonderful, when we meet again, kiss, hug, and love in the greatest place ever—beloved heaven.

Let's Be Glad
and No More Sad

(Man)

I cried a tear for you, my dear. It is so clear you don't want to be near, so I am now in so much fear. If only you could come back here, I would be in a world of cheer. I would be so glad, but I know that won't happen. So now I am so sad. Why are you so bad? Why can't you be glad instead of all so sad? We don't have to be mad, so let's work real hard to be glad and no more sad. We will have lots of fun and maybe a son 'til our life on earth is done.

I Had a Million Things to Tell You

(Man)

I had a million things to tell you, but I will be darned if I know where to start. Every one of them is oh so very, very important! So I must first say I love you, love you from now and to eternity. If I ever lost you again, my life, my world would be no more. It would not exist because you are a saint, a lover, already so outstanding. There is no replacement. You were made in a golden mold, fashioned and engineered by the greatest One up above. How could I ever treat you other than the saint, the precious angel you truly are. So I will work day and night 'til our special love is molded into an unbreakable, very precious love that will continue on for the great and beautiful forever.

Christmas

(Woman)

I saw the glory of Christmas, the presents coming in, the presents going out, and the beautiful Christmas music that rocks through buildings, houses, and cars. It appears everyone is filled with so much happiness and laughter on the great Jesus' birthday. It is the most joyful day of the year, our Lord Jesus' birthday. All is well, pure, and sweet. The poor, the rich, the old the young, everyone is in boundless love and glory. If this is just a sample of glorious heaven, how great it must be to enter God's great kingdom up above with all the angels singing and endless joy, music, and kindness in our world forever and ever.

If There Were a World
Where Only Love Existed

(Man)

If there were a world where only love existed, what a precious world that would be. I would hold my darling's hand and dance and kiss and hug her as we glided around the dance floor. We would sit down and tell each other how much our precious love for each other is, so very outstanding. I would smile at her. She would smile back. We would wink at each other and hug and kiss. It would seem our love grows longer and longer, stronger, and stronger. I could not let her go. She would not let me go, so we are in love so outstanding that we don't ever want to be separated, just locked in a lovelock forever in a very precious world where only love exists.

My Darling Wife, Loved By All

(Man)

That girl is on the phone. She is always on that phone. I love her so much and want to talk to her so much, but she is always on the phone. I guess it's just because she is loved so much and by so many. It is so very hard to call her. She makes my life, my love, so complete just to talk to my precious darling who is loved and cherished by so very many people. Old or young, it makes no difference. She is so very, very special. She is loved by so very many, many people. Everyone wants to talk to her because she is so smart, kind, and wonderful. No one wants to put down the phone, just talk and talk to my very special darling who is in a unique class, a special person, loved and adored by one and all. I must be the luckiest man in all the world to have been chosen by a lady so outstanding as my darling wife, a lady of so many, many unified qualities.

Our Precious Daughters

(Man)

That little girl of mine, she is so cute, so sweet, so wonderful. She is the apple of our eye, Mommy and me. She is a little three-foot, beautiful bundle of the greatest love we have ever seen. Oh, how very special and very lucky Mommy and I are to have had that little tiny sweetheart bundle of joy she gives us day after day. We have to be so very special to have had such a glorious, little, precious daughter who gives Mommy and me so much happiness every precious day of our wonderful lives. We are so sad when she is sick, but a world of happiness when she's well and spreading all her precious love. There is no greater happiness than that great love she gives to us each day of her very precious life for which we are oh so thankful!

That is how dad and mom feel about all four of their precious daughters. Cathy, Lisa, Chris and Laura whom we all love so very, very much and so very happy and thankful for each and every one of them.

Cathy, Lisa, Chris and Laura

In my first marriage I had four beautiful, smart, lovely little daughters whom love me and mom very, very much. They grew up beautiful, smart, lovely ladies. Cathy is married with children. She is manager of American Legion Post 69. Her husband Sherman is the Commander of the Post. Lisa is a Mary Kay Sales representative with children. She is married to Raymond who is a heavy equipment operator. Chris has her own cleaning business, has a son and helps in the American Legion. Laura does pay roll for Matozol Casino, has children, and is married to Hubert CEO of the Casino. They all have a happy and wonderful life which me and mom, are so very happy and proud of them and thankful and will help them every day of their very precious lives. We are also proud, loving, and thankful of all our precious grandsons and granddaughters. They swell our hearts with endless joy day after day.

We Have Found Each Other

(Man)

There will always be another hill or mountain to climb or another valley to go through or another raging river to cross that will all be worth it gladly when I finally find my precious darling. I know and feel she is out there somewhere, some very special place. I know I will find her. I will leave no rock unturned and no path untraveled 'til that precious, beautiful darling is locked in my loving arms. I will work day and night and search everywhere 'til I find my special darling. I was running in the park, and this beautiful lady was charging toward me. Somehow we collided into each other as our eyes locked together. We both knew in that second, that second of time oh so very special, we were meant for each other in a lifetime of pure, sweet, immaculate love.

The Killer Mountain

(Man)

On a cold and icy cliff on a brutal mountain in Alaska, they were climbing and already knew the nasty mountain had taken several lives. Their goal was to reach the summit at all costs. The severe cold and blowing snow made it almost impossible to climb another foot on that severe, icy mountainside, but these were some of the meanest, toughest men in all the world, who refused to be beaten. Their hands were almost frozen, and their faces like that of ice as they plowed up the seemingly unclimbable icy mountain. They heard, as they climbed, the screeching, murderous cry, as some of the climbers fell to their death from the mountain. They started with eight climbers. Now they were down to four. They had lost half of their precious climbers. Then to their great surprise, they saw the mountaintop, the summit, as overwhelming joy entered their minds and bodies, but they still had the very dangerous descent down the treacherous mountain. They were men of steel and felt they would make it all the way as they fought on in the almost impossible mission to victory and to the bottom of the vicious mountain.

Searching for My Precious Love

(Woman)

I will climb mountains, down valleys, and then to oceans 'til I find my special darling. I will leave no stones unturned 'til I reach my goal of finding you. I know you are out there somewhere, someplace. I don't think you are hiding. I will search here and there and everywhere 'til I find you and see you, so handsome, sexy, and so kind and wonderful, in my dreams every night. Once I find you, then truly will I take you everywhere and love you like the precious angel I know you truly are. I will make it a very special point every day to treat and love you like the most special darling you truly are.

The Greatest Jesus

(Man)

The beautiful evening, the awesome night, the world rocks with happiness. Our Savior Jesus Christ is born. He shines and glows with glory in His little stable where everyone looks on, and all the angels are praising His glory. The Blessed Mother looks with glowing love at her Son, the beloved Jesus, who is here to save the world. He is the precious Savior for whom we all have been waiting. All the people have been gathering to get a glimpse of the immaculate Jesus. We can feel the vibrations coming from His wondrous mind and body in the form of eternal peace. This is the greatest day in all the world, for our beloved Savior has come to us here on earth, but a few terrible people take our precious Jesus from us. Then a little later, the miraculous happens. Our love-bound Savior Jesus rises to His sacred home in heaven where we all hope and pray we will someday join Him.

No Sun Today, But We Had Fun

(Woman)

Where have you gone, Mr. Sun, on this cloudy day? Are you hiding in the fluffier clouds in the sky above? Oh, how I want to go out and play on a sunshiny day! As I look out the window on this cloudy, dreary day, it makes me so sad, so I must play inside today.

Then all of a sudden I hear the thunder and rain comes falling down, and my darling mommy says, "Do you want to play in the rain today?"

Oh how excited I become with my raincoat on! I played with my little girlfriend next door. It was a very special day of oh so much fun, and we were sad no more that Mr. Sun did not come out today.

Will My Precious Angel Say Yes?

(Man)

If I knew you would say no to me, I would cry a lifetime of tears for you, my very special angel that I have known for a long, long time, but I have not had the guts or the courage to ask you out. I guess it is because it would hurt me oh so much if you said no, because we are such great friends, and we like each other a lot. So I must get the strength I need to ask that precious angel out with me. Today is that special day I will ask her out, and I hope and pray she says yes.

So I ask, "Will you please go with me on a date?" and to my great surprise she says, (Woman) "Yes," (Man/Woman) and the wonderful miracle happened. We fell in love and had a fine marriage and wonderful family.

I Had a Feeling

(Man)

I had a feeling I would find my one true love. I know it's only a feeling, but when I woke up this morning, I had that precious feeling you were near, close, and dear, that I might have a glimpse of you somewhere. I am making my coffee. I get that feeling you are so close, but I've had that feeling so many times before, and nothing happened, to my great despair. I look here and there and everywhere with no results, just that terrible wanting and overbearing sadness. I don't give up. I can't and I won't, for my life is not complete without your love. I am just a hollow shell of a man who must secure a special love that you must have for me. So I will search day and night, high and low, because I know that love of yours will someday be mine. I stopped at traffic, and the young lady started to cross the street. I grabbed her back from that fast-moving truck. I looked at her. She looked at me and knew I saved her from a terrible accident.

(Man/Woman) We continued to look at each other, our eyes locked together as our hearts beat furiously, and we knew at once our love was pure, sweet, and secure. We have finally met, and what a glorious time it is, for we will now live, love, and cherish each other in a lifetime of endless love and happiness.

God, Jesus

(Man)

Jesus here, Jesus there, and Jesus everywhere. He is our warrior, our leader, our one and only true commander. He helps us every day of our lives, in sickness, wellness, and in danger, in all the many functions of our life. He guides and steers us down our precious life of glory. We believe in You and all Your works and miracles and kindness. We pray to Him, we lean on Him, and we adore Him, our beloved Jesus. (Man/Woman) He is our bright and shining light in all the many good and bad situations. We feel the coming of the Lord, we feel Him by our side, in our dreams, everywhere. The eye in the sky is our Jesus, our Lord and Savior. He is our world, our life, our existence. He will be our navigator through all our worldly problems. We must love Him, cherish Him, and hold Him on the highest pedestal, so we can live forever with Jesus in his beloved Heaven up above.

Just One More Time

(Man)

Just one more time, one more beautiful, precious time with you, my sweet and unbelievable one and only darling, will make my love and happiness excel in a world of everlasting love that could last forever and ever.

(Woman) Every time we have ever touched, loved, and been together, we fall deeper and deeper and longer and longer in an immaculate love and cycle that can never, ever be broken. It is imprinted on both of our minds and bodies to last now and through eternity

(Man) It seems your luscious kiss, hug, laugh, and kindness increase two-fold more and more.

(Woman) I don't see how it is earthly possible for two loves to increase so overwhelmingly. It feels almost our love inside could explode in a million, billion tiny, little, gorgeous balls of love.

(Man/Woman) Just one more time, one more day, one more year, and more of the finest life two loving people could ever have, now and throughout our precious forever life.

My Little Chevy Pickup Truck

(Man)

I zig, I zag, driving my little 1995 Chevy pickup truck through the heavy traffic to work. If it's warm or cold, the little Chevy pickup truck purrs right along, leaves other cars and trucks in a cloud of dust and gas fumes. Rolling, rolling down the road in my little 1995 Chevy pickup truck all shiny red and oh so pretty. People look at the pretty truck as it zips by, and I know they wish they were driving that little red 1995 Chevy pickup truck of mine. It is a beauty. People say, "How much do you want for your little Chevy pickup truck?" and I say, "I love it oh so much. I can't sell it." I will keep it as long as it zips and zags in and out of traffic and down the road it does roar 'til it's destination it does reach.

Your Special Love Song

(Man)

Let me sing to you, my sweetheart. I want to sing a song of love to you. I want to make it oh so special that it will bring tears running from your eyes down your very, very beautiful face like falling rain. I want to sing it so beautifully that you will remember it for a very special lifetime. I want your very special song to be so great it will make you (Man/Woman) sing right along with me as I sing it to you. It will make you dance and scream because the words will be so beautifully special and consuming. You will inhale and love every word as we sing together that very special love song I have written and sing to you. I want it to hold you so intensely you will let the song and music vibrate through your heart, mind, and body as the greatest of music and love story, every song to a sweetheart so very, very special as you, my beloved darling, my endless love.

Survival

(Man)

I am in the wild Alaskan mountains, and I am lost. My food and water have diminished. I hear the wolves howling and coming closer, and I know they are hungry, looking for food, and would like to take me down. I will fight ferociously with only one intent—to kill and survive. I must find my friend's cabin before darkness comes. I see a huge grizzly in my path ahead. I must deter him from any action, so I grab my rifle and fire a round, and the bear charges off.

The cold, fierce temperature is almost unbearable. My hands and feet seem almost frozen, and my strength has withered. I am so hungry and thirsty I can hardly take another step. I reach back and, to my surprise, obtain more strength. Then the great miracle happens. I see in the distance smoke coming out of the chimney in my friend's little log cabin. I feel I am an extremely lucky person to have survived that long distance journey to safety.

My Precious Angel
Come From Heaven

(Man)

I have a precious angel sent from up above and that precious angel is to be my wife. You are my one and only angel who had to come from up above. There is no angel like you down here on earth because you are so very special. Everyone can see and know you are truly not from this world. You had to have been sent down from heaven because you are so very, very special. Everyone sees the greatness pour out of your mind and body. I have a precious angel from up above, and that precious angel is my wife. You have a religious tone, spirit, and being that has never been found here on earth. Oh, what a very lucky person I must be for you to choose me as your husband! It has to make me the luckiest person in all the world. My beloved angel has a way, a being not seen on earth before. I feel I am so outclassed, so far behind her type of sweet, loving, spiritual greatness.

(Man/Woman) We know we will have the greatest husband and wife combination and family thereafter. We will work day and night to keep our precious love supreme and unbreakable. I have a precious angel sent from up above, and that precious angel is to be my wife.

My Little Tom Cat

(Woman)

I thought I heard a tom cat whining at my door. He sounded so hungry, so lonesome, and so tired. I went to check on him. As I opened the door, the little kitten jumped right inside my house. He just stood there blinking his pretty brown eyes at me. I held out my hand, and he came running to me. He was so cold and shaking. I fixed him a bowl of warm milk, and he began to drink. He later followed me everywhere I went. It seemed as though we were meant forever to be each other's best of friends. I fixed him a little box with a blanket by the stove so he could be warm. He purred on with a little whimper. When I go to work, he looks out the window with sadness, and when I return, he is so happy, rubbing against my leg. It looks like both of us have found a lot of happiness together in our little house of love.

The Family

(Man)

I knew you were the one when our eyes locked together and my heart beat so profoundly with overwhelming happiness. You are so pretty, sexy, and so sweet. Your words seemed to melt the thoughts in my mind. When we talk, our one question to each other seemed the same. I could never find a love that ever comes close to the love I have for you. It is so pure, so sweet, and so everlasting. I am sure it comes from God in Heaven. This immaculate love is unbelievable to every fiber of my body. We now have such a wonderful, loving, precious family, the spitting image of my beloved wife. Such a truly great and precious family, I thank our savior Jesus everyday and night for all he has done for us. I truly feel I must be the luckiest man in all the world to have found you, loved you, because you are my world, my everything.

I Knew Our Love Was Forever

(Woman)

I felt the lining of my heart give way when you said we were through. How could you say such sad and terrible words? I will not take those bad words for gospel, because I know somehow, some way, I will win you back to me because we were once the greatest pair of lovers this world had ever seen. We were truly inseparable, united together as one. I will do my very best with all my persuading ways, and you will once again be mine. I am enticing you now with all of my love tactics, and I can see it is weakening you. I see you are now unsure, and my love is bouncing off you in so many ways.

You are now smiling and looking at me and loving me in a very sexy, wanting way. You come closer and cannot stop. You scream with love to me, saying, "I love you darling, you are all the world to me. I am sorry I could never leave. Your love is binding and holding and securing. Your love is all the world to me and will truly last forever and ever."

Wandering Willema

(Man)

Where have you gone, Wandering Willema? Have you met another in your wandering ways? I am so lonesome and sad since you have wandered away from me. Wandering Willema, won't you please wander back to me. I feel I could wander to you, but I think we are wandering in different directions.

(Man/Woman) I hope some day when wandering we will wander back together again and will no longer be sad and miserable because we have wandered back together, Wandering Willema, and our lives will be complete with endless love and happiness and no more wandering for you or for me.

My Darling's Terrible Accident

(Man)

I cried a tear and more and more came down like falling rain from my face. I could not see. I only wept. *Where is my love, my life, my only one? Where have you gone?* The unending torment had me paralyzed in endless grief. I could not move, eat or think. I did not know what happened to my beloved darling wife. There was no word, no message for her leaving. I checked here and there and everywhere with no result. I cannot believe what happened to my precious darling.

Then I heard that terrible, remorseful newscast that there was a severe accident on that icy road on Route 5 that took my darling's life. I will be in the greatest of pain and agony until we meet in the great hereafter, where only love exists.

The Great One

(Man)

Sweet and wonderful Jesus is born in a manger in Bethlehem. Today our Lord and Savior is with us at last. The whole world rejoices. We have our great religious Father to guide us spiritually for the rest of our lives and thereafter. When He was a child, He seemed like any other. As He grew older, we saw His precious teachings take place, and His various miracles were performed. All of us were in awe and knew He was our Savior and our leader, beloved God Jesus.

(Man/Woman) Then some very bad and terrible rulers didn't cherish His love and teachings and forced Him to carry a large cross up the hillside and nailed Him to the cross. He later died and was entombed, but on the third beautiful day, He arose from the tomb and ascended into His precious Kingdom in Heaven where we all hope and pray we will join Jesus in His land of greatness in that wonderful hereafter up above.

In Memory of My Precious Wife

(Man)

In memory of my precious darling, who I miss day and night, year after year, who left me oh so early in our marriage. She was so sick from that terrible cancer we could not conquer. So I am sure she is with the great One up above, standing in the doorway to precious Heaven, waiting for my arrival, to continue our endless love, which will explode in the great and wonderful Heaven up above. It will rock and roll and blaze in endless love up above in the great hereafter. It will be so admired by everyone, that very special love of yours and mine.

Right or Wrong

(Woman)

Right or wrong, day by day, I know you are the one who is right for me. People say, "He is wrong for you."

I have never seen a man so good, so wonderful, so right for me. He is the one, that very special one to be my loving husband. I will cherish and love him as he does me—all the right things and very few wrong things. He always puts me right at the top, never wrong. I will love him right at the top and above as my Mr. Right and not wrong. We will have a life of endless rights and very few wrongs because it's very real. We are truly meant for each other the right way and in love with each other for a beautiful lifetime. There is no greater love than the love we have for each other.

"Lean on Me," Says Precious Jesus

(Man)

"Lean on me," says precious Jesus, "and I will keep and guide you through the troubled pathway of life. So you will have fewer problems, lean on me. I will be your guiding light, your pathway to safety. Do not hesitate. Lean on me. I am your leader, your helper, your guidance through the many troubles you may encounter in this world of ours. So don't take any chances. Lean on me. I will be your navigator through all your earthly problems. Lean on me. I know your safe passage through all the troubles and problems to which you may come to, so lean on me."

(Man/Woman) "I am your guidance, the eye in the sky, your safety to the special way to My beloved kingdom. Lean on me, I love you one and all and I will take you up above with me forever. So lean on me, now and forever. Lean on me," says our beloved Jesus.

I Will Meet My Love Soon

(Woman)

You are my guiding light. You are the compass of my direction. Without you I am on a shipwrecked island in the South Pacific. I will wander aimlessly here and there and everywhere 'til our two beautiful loves collide together as a very precious one. I know what you look like, all pretty, kind, and sweet. I have seen you in my dreams and thoughts hundreds of times. I know somewhere, someplace we will be drawn together, and that very priceless miracle will take place. I can tell it won't be long because, as I think of you, my heart, mind, and body seem to be in a very, very precious lovelock or trance built and designed for precious you and you only.

Billy Boy

(Woman)

Where have you gone, Billy Boy? Oh, how we miss you so very much, Billy Boy. Your smiley face, your brilliant laughter, your overwhelming kindness. We miss you so very much every day. You were so kind and considerate. We love you so much. You are all the world to all of us, Billy Boy. Days, weeks, and months go by as we worry for your return. You were the sunshine in our hearts and the glory in our minds for so many loved ones. I am now sure you are cherished even more up above as we now find out you have died in that terrible war in Vietnam. Your family will miss you so terribly, and America thanks you so very much for your sad death and long service to help protect the great U.S.A. Billy Boy's outstanding combat ability against the enemy earned him the military's highest, most coveted award, the Congressional Medal of Honor.

I Will Continue to Win Her Over

(Man)

I had a chance with you, a very special chance with you. I smiled at you, and received no smile back from you. So stupid me, I walked away and didn't say hi, just walked away. She could have been that special one, but I just walked away. As I think back, I sure hope I get another chance. I will smile and ask and do whatever it takes to get that pretty lady's attention. If I have to practice day and night to win her over, then that is what I must do.

Here she comes all bright and oh, what a knockout she so truly is. I smile again and say hi.

She gives me a big oh, smiles and says, "I am sorry for not smiling or saying hi."

I ask, "Would you please go out with me?"

She said, "Oh yes."

I could not believe it. I have won the starting battle, and I will continue to win that precious lady over to me.

I Wandered Aimlessly

(Man)

I ran the terribly burning wall of endless hell, and precious Jesus pulled me out. I wandered aimlessly into the valley of no return. I had no desire, no happiness as I entered deeper and deeper into the bottomless dark down under of the valley of no return. I felt beaten and defeated in the deep, dark down under and wandered aimlessly deeper and deeper into that miserable valley of no return. I ran the terrible burning wall of endless hell, and precious Jesus pulled me out. Then I saw that beautiful lady in the distance. At once I felt reborn, new, a man with reason and hope as I pulled, gouged, yanked and beat my way out—thanks to Jesus—of that miserable valley of no return into life, happiness, and precious living, as that beautiful, very sexy lady said to me, (Woman) "Can I help you? How are you? Are you alright?"

(Man) I felt like never before—bright, alive, and glorious as she pulled me. (Man/Woman) Thanks to Jesus from that miserable valley of no return, to love, life, and endless happiness. We almost instantly fell in love, which lasted a lifetime, and we hope and pray into the great and beautiful hereafter.

My Darling is For the Best

(Man)

In my past years, you were the best, smartest, prettiest, sexiest, and the most wonderful lady in all the world. In these present years, you are still the most precious, greatest, and outstanding, finest angel in all the wide, wide world. I have searched a lifetime, far and wide, high and low, and I never ever have seen a match to even come close to my beloved darling. I feel I am so outmatched, so out-classed, but oh so thankful to be the luckiest man in this beautiful, wide and wonderful world in which we live and love. For my darling to choose me above all the rest is truly unbelievable, and it makes me the most thankful man ever.

Our Old and New Love Bits and Pieces

(Man)

It's just bits and pieces of an old love affair. I see bits here and pieces there. What a beautiful love we would have if we could get all those bits and pieces together. I am sure it would be that supreme love affair we once had. It was so great. Now there are just bits and pieces of an old love affair. I think if both of us tried to take all those bits and pieces and put them together, it may even be better than that special love affair we had before instead of just those terrible little bits and pieces of that old love we once had before. So I will grab some pieces, and she will get some bits, and (Man/Woman) if we work real hard putting those bits and pieces together, what a miraculous love affair we both feel it will be, and far more superior to that we once had. No more bits and pieces, just bits and pieces together in an endless love affair.

My Angel Came From Heaven

(Man)

I have a special angel sent from God above, an angel, a very special angel, to be my precious wife. You can tell right away she is an angel by the way she looks so saintly, so pure, so precise. I can't believe that special angel sent from God is now my wife. Oh, how could a man like me be so honored to receive that very special someone to be my angel wife! It is so clear she's not from this world, but was definitely sent from God's great Heaven. It is oh so clear when you see or talk to her, listen to her, she was sent from the great up above. Oh how proud, thankful, and lucky I am. I will cherish, love, and adore my angel to eternity.

U.S.A. Number One

(Man)

They come, some older, some younger, to fight, to die for this our beloved United States of America. To fight, to protect our great and wonderful U.S.A., we will fight our way to victory in the air, on mountaintops, oceans, valleys, and forests. It makes no difference where or who we fight. We will excel, do our very best to keep our beautiful U.S.A. always everywhere and forever number one, the very best always. Even though we lose so many of our precious American soldiers, we must always be victorious. Even though we lose a lot of our beloved soldiers in war, it is always necessary to never surrender or give up or quit, but to push on to victory and to always keep the U.S.A. undefeated, never to lose, always to win and always to protect.

I Won You Over, Darling

(Woman)

Could it be special you, I have finally fallen in love with you? Oh, precious you, so beautiful, sweet, and wonderful, I feel I have finally won you over. It was not an easy battle. I worked so very hard to gain your confidence, your precious trust. It was oh so hard a battle to win you over, but now I see all the beautiful, gorgeous benefits of my precious victory to secure your heart together with mine. It seems now we talk, love, and act as a beloved one to go on united in our love mold to continue always, so it will last for a precious forever and into the great thereafter.

Terrible War in Korea

(Man)

I remembered when I left to fight a terrible war in Korea. My darling looked so pretty, sexy, and so sweet in our little house in Ohio. How I miss her oh so much now that I've been fighting this terrible war in Korea. I pray to God I will survive this miserable war to return home to my darling. I have had five tours in the roughest, meanest of combats with the army in that cruel war in Korea. I had a lot of close calls from the nasty, sneaky enemy. I felt God must have guided me to safety in so many ways. We lost so many soldiers. I felt my time was up in so many battles, yet I fought through. The physical and mental cruelty is sometimes almost unbearable, yet you cannot stop. You must push on to victory for this great and wonderful America to protect our country, our people, our beautiful world. I am battered and bruised physically and mentally for this toughest, roughest war in Korea, and thanks be to God I made it. Now I am on an airplane headed home to my sweetheart in Ohio, and freedom roars with victory and overwhelming happiness.

Our Very Special Love

(Man)

I found a love so pure, so sweet, never found here on earth. It is so unbelievable two like me and her could fall in love so strong, so solid, a love like ours never seen before. Oh so special is our love, pure and immaculate. I feel it is in a special class of its own, which will last on and on and will truly be unbreakable but will grow and grow into the greatest love affair two very special people could have, cherish, or hold, so outstanding, and we will work with joy and covet it now and make it grow even stronger and more beautiful now and 'til our time on earth has ended, and then in the very special hereafter.

Beloved Jesus

(Woman)

I see You in my far off distance and feel You in my fast-beating heart. My love for You increases day by day and is so overwhelming and so sincere. You are my life, my love, my very being. I hope and pray You have Your precious eyes locked on me, so someday you will take me up above when my life on earth is finished. I know I am no saint. I have failed You in so many ways, but my love grows stronger and stronger for You, precious Jesus, as time goes by. I am helping others, trying to do better, so I can only hope and pray You will forgive my many faults and mistakes and take me up to your beloved Heaven and let me live with You forever in a greatness unbelievable to all your precious followers.

My Precious Angel Sent From God

(Man)

I had an angel, a very special angel sent from God in most beautiful heaven. Oh, that angel, that very special angel sent from God was to be my wife. Oh, how could that angel sent from God's great Heaven be my wife? I am truly not worthy of that precious caliber of greatness because she outclasses me. She is so much better than me. I look at her, and I am instantly in love. You can tell right away she is not from this world but definitely from up above in God's great Heaven. I will work so very hard to love, to cherish, to adore her for a lifetime of endless love and respect for God's great angel and my precious wife.

I Will Work Hard
For Your Return

(Woman)

I cried a tear, a special tear on my loss of you. I don't know why you left me. All I know is tears come down my face like falling rain. I will search high and low for your return. Could it be our love has faded and my attention could be fading and slipping for our precious love? I need more consideration, more trust, and love for you because I cannot lose you. I know you are all the world to me. I would be oh so sad if you did not return to me. I will work so preciously hard to get you back to me for I would be lost and beaten without you, precious darling. I would have no life without you, so I will get you back, and our love will be the greatest ever.

Great America

(Man)

Great America, oh how I love you, respect you, and adore you, for your fight for freedom, justice, equality, and love for all, the great and wonderful U.S.A. We will join you left and right, front and center, in any conflict or war we deem necessary, with our famous military—Army, Navy, Marines, Air Force, and Coast Guard.

(Man/Woman) There is no country to match America in strength, power, and greatness. We must always continue to build, to strengthen, and to keep the U.S.A. at the top. Our beloved soldiers every day in all of our military work day and night to keep us above all other countries' forces, and thanks to all the living soldiers, the maimed and the many deceased who have given their precious lives to keep this great United States of America number one in every respect and never to falter, so we can always remain the greatest, most outstanding country now and forever, remaining number one in every way, whose freedom, justice, and equality are forever and ever.

A Moment So Special
That Lives Forever

(Woman)

This is the moment, that special moment for which we have been looking. This is the moment our two special loves will unite as a very special moment in time—a moment so wonderful it screams with beautiful joy. This is the moment of unending happiness, just everlasting love and kindness. You and me in that screaming moment of pure love that can't be silenced, just roars on and on. Everyone is watching and cheering as that precious moment of love gets bigger and larger and everyone says oh, how can that be? It must happen because it is a pure mountain of love in a very special moment of endless love that is unbreakable, that will live on and on through that very special moment of forever and ever.

Take a Moment in Time

(Man)

In the first moment of time I saw her, I fell in love with her, head over heels. In that very first moment of time, I knew she was the one, the very special one to love, to cherish, and have for all time, not just for a moment. I asked her to go dancing with me, and to my great surprise, she said, "Yes, I would love to," in that moment of time.

(Man) Take a moment of time and let me tell you how much I love you, how pretty, sexy, and kind you are. I take a moment as my heart is beating out of control with pure love. I had a moment, a loving moment in time. I will never, ever forget this precious moment. I can't work or sleep or eat because, in this extremely special moment of time, I have fallen in love with my precious, beloved darling. I see your pretty face, your gorgeous body, and so wonderful personality. In this moment of time, I wonder if her feelings are the same as mine.

(Woman) We danced and danced ever so close in this moment of time. I wondered if he might pop that beautiful question in this moment of time. We stopped dancing and went to the table. In that moment of time, he took one knee and asked me, (Man) "Will you please be my greatest moment in time and marry me?"

(Woman) I jumped up and smiled as I uttered the precious, "Yes, my darling."

(Man/Woman) In this beautiful moment in time as our lives unite as one in a gorgeous moment in time, now and to eternity, in this very special moment of time, we give each other everlasting glorious love.

Loss to Regain

(Man)

The tortured tendons of my heart seemed to explode when you said our love was finished. How could you be so cruel to utter those most hated words a man could ever hear? I could not believe you said those terrible words: We are finished. Have you found another more precious to your wanting? I thought our love was special and supreme, but somewhere I must have failed you, dropped the ball, or did not have enough consideration. I hope somehow, somewhere you will give me one more unbelievable chance to reenter your precious heart and live with you now and into the great future of happiness for a very special forever.

My Precious Dog Brownie

(Woman)

I had a brown dog. He was my guide, my protector, and my best friend. His name was Brownie. Brownie and I went everywhere together. We were inseparable, united together as one. Brownie protected me from bears, wolves, mountain lions, and many other dangers, or I would not be alive today. So I thank my dog, my very special dog and best friend, Brownie, to be united together with the greatest friend, protector, a woman could ever have, but now every day I am oh so sad my Brownie is here no more.

Brownie has left me 'cause of old age. He is tired from protecting me and the work he has performed so magnificently, but most of all, the precious, most overwhelming love we had for each other, he will carry on up above 'til we meet again in the great hereafter.

Jesus, Our Everything

(Woman)

I have a precious angel sent from God most beloved in Heaven. Jesus has an immaculate mind and body, and His super way He controls the world and everything else. Without Him, we are nothing. He is our life, our love, and our very happiness. For without precious Jesus, we are lost and defeated, for He is our everything, beautiful Jesus so supreme, our guiding light, our world, and everything else. We lean on Him, we trust Him, we pray to Him, and we adore Him, for He is our everything. Every day of our life, He helps and guides us through the precious pathway of life. If we are good, kind, and wonderful, He will be waiting in the doorway of His beloved Heaven to a place unbelievable we can only imagine.

I Miss You So Much

(Man)

Oh how I miss you, darling, when you left me yesterday, bound for Heaven. I'll see and hear you here and there and everywhere. Your beautiful face appears, and so much sadness sets in. The tears come down like falling rain upon my face. It is almost unbearable to continue on, but I feel you by my side, hand in hand. I go to work, which is so hard because my memory wanders back to you, my precious darling. I feel you are in the truck, chatting with me always. My life has crushed to a standstill in memory of you always. What a precious, sweet, and wonderful wife you were to me. I know I had to be the luckiest man in all the world to be married to you, my little angel who has left for Heaven. I count the days, the months, the years 'til we reunite in that beautiful kingdom up above. I have a lifetime of endless love to give to you, my darling, and not a day to lose when we must preciously meet again.

Love You

(Woman)

Won't you let me love you, kiss you, hug you like no one else can do? I promise no one, and you have never been loved like the love I am going to give you. I will adore and cherish you right up to the maximum your sweet and wonderful heart can withstand. My love to you will be so very special. It will be almost too extreme for you to handle. There will be times you will say, "Stop, I cannot take any more of your precious love. Please, let's take a moment for my heart to recover from the love you have been giving me, so endearing. My heart, my body and mind cannot accept that much brilliant love your love bestows upon me. Give me a breather, and we once again will reunite in a love neither one of us could imagine, believe, or dream, a love truly two loving couples have never endured or received, which the two of us have created, which is truly one of a very special kind."

Joaquin Bareatta

(Man)

You are my world, my everlasting happiness, so won't you please be my Joaquin Bareatta and love me for a lifetime and thereafter? Won't you walk and talk to me and kiss and hug me and tell me all the love you have for me, and I will preciously do the same to you, my sweetheart, Joaquin Bareatta? I want to marry you and have a wonderful, loving life in all the precious years we have together, and I think we will create a great and special family with you to love and cherish. So please by my Joaquin Bareatta, and we'll love each other forever in this beautiful world. Won't you spend now and all the years of love and happiness with me, my beautiful, lovely darling. I want to live with you eternally, my luscious, sexy Joaquin Bareatta. I want to adore you with both of our hearts beating as one so purely forever because you are the rock of my foundation, you are my everything, my beloved Joaquin Bareatta, and after death I want to follow you to God's great kingdom, my one and only. So please be my life, my world, my everything, for without you I am nothing. With you I have everything, my precious, beloved darling Joaquin Bareatta.

I Will Know
My Precious Sweetheart

(Man)

I will know you are the only one, my heart will stop beating for a moment or two, my eyes will be locked in a constant stare on your beautiful face. I will know you are the one because I have seen and memory-banked your beautiful face and smile in my dreams each night. I will know it's precious you when I look at you with my mouth open in awe. I will see your beautiful smile mold into mine, a precious one. I will know when you speak the soft, beautiful words floating out of your mouth like that of a beloved angel. It will all come together when we look at each other, touch, and miraculously kiss, which binds and seals our love together as a very, very special one in a million to last forever on earth and the beautiful heavens above. A love one in a billion engineered in heaven as the angels sing so beautiful in the beloved sky above.

Here We Are

(Woman)

Here we are, you and me, the two most in love people in all the world. Here we are so happy, so content, so deeply in love, you and me, giving thanks for all we have, love, and respect. Here we are in our beautiful world of love, you and me, in our little house of love. Here we are, everyone looking at our beautiful love for each other, surrounded by so many loved ones, friends, and family. Here we are. We work, we play, we love because we have so much, so thankful, because we are in this big, wide, wonderful world and so in love. Here we are. We don't need to wish for anything because we are so deeply in love. We have our precious love. We have everything, and we are oh so very thankful. We have it all and hope all others have the same.

My Precious Kitty and Doggy

(Woman)

My little kitty and doggy are all the world to me. They wake me up each morning, oh so happy. I am delighted to see their smiley faces as I wrestle with them in the brisk morning air. They are always so happy and excited to see me, as I am to see them. They make my day, my world complete, running hear and there and by my side with pure, sweet love. I would be so lost without my little sweet and wonderful little kitty and doggy. That is what I named them, and they love it. We love each other to the max and above, each day of our precious lives, and then we'll start all over tomorrow and hope it lasts so long on and on with pure love and kindness.

Oh, Where Have We Gone?

(Man)

Oh, where oh where have we gone? We have gone so, so far apart. Our love is no more. Oh, where have we gone to no man's land? We were once so much in love. We were inseparable. Now it seems we are wandering aimlessly. There is no rhyme or reason. Oh, where have we gone and our precious love we once held as gospel? We don't know if this happened, our precious loss of love, day by day or at once. Oh, where have we gone? We are still together but oh so very far apart. What has happened to our love, which we once thought was so sincere? Oh, where have we gone?

(Man/Woman) As we were walking down the street, a bolt of lightning hit a tree in front of us and knocked it down. We were in a beautiful, loving trance or daze. As we awakened so slowly, it seemed like a heavenly awakening we never encountered before. We were once madly in love like "oh, where have we gone" never happened, and we are keeping this beautiful madly in love forever encounter everlasting in our hearts and minds.

I Have Wronged You, My Precious Darling, But I Will Restore Our Love Forever

(Man)

I am sorry. Please forgive me. I have wronged you. I don't know why I have been so careless and so bad. Please forgive me. I am oh so sorry. Please let me pay you back, asking for forgiveness, kindness, and the greatest of consideration. I will be so careful, so kind, and so loving to never let this happen again. Oh, please forgive me. I have failed you, treated you so wrongly. I will pay you back with overwhelming love and great consideration. I will work so hard to restore the love of ours I have damaged. I will always show you the maximum love, kindness, and respect you truly deserve. I will never, ever falter or betray the very precious love I have for you, for you are my one true love, my very, very beloved sweetheart. I will make it my life's work to give a supreme love to you that you have never seen before, which will hold us together as one in this endless lovelock forever.

Market

(Man)

I wake up in the morning, and the stock market is down three hundred points. I get a cup of coffee, and the market turns around and is up two hundred points now. How can I make any money in these wild swings in the market? Some days I am up two dollars, and in a minute, down seventy-five dollars. Oh, where can I put my money to make a good living? I must put money here and money there, so I am truly diversified and don't have to worry about all the ups and downs in the market because it is up most of the time to make money, and that will pay off.

A Precious Love
That Won't Be Broken Ever

(Man)

I felt you so close, so near and so dear, but how could that be, because you left me? Even at times, I see you, hear you, there and everywhere. Is it because our love was so strong, so stout, it was truly unbreakable? Even at night, I am sleeping and dreaming you are right there with me. Oh, what a precious feeling it is to know you are with me so much in love, so happy and content, it even softens the awakening when you're not there and have gone to beautiful Heaven, waiting for me at the beautiful doorway to God's great Heaven. It must be our love was so supreme it's not broken or damaged, even in death. A love so pure, so wonderful, I feel you with me in so much love and contentment. I know it will blossom even more in the beautiful Heaven above where we will reunite, love, and cherish forever in endless love.

Our Precious
Love Is Meant Forever

(Man)

Do not leave me for that other dude. He will not love you like I do. He will treat you mean, and then he will dump you. The love I have for you is so true and sincere. His love for you is just make-believe. He can only love himself. What a waste his love for you would be. You are way too precious, so loving, and so sweet. You must have the love I have for you, which is so immaculate it will hold you in a love circle that could never be broken. His is just an imitation of that precious, overwhelming love I have for you. I see I have won you over. You are heading straight for me with arms extended, lips quivering, as I press my lips to yours. You seem to scream, yell, and quake as our beloved kiss grows stronger and longer and seems to last for hours, just proving our sacred love was meant to be now and into the great and precious forever.

Shame on Me, Immaculate Jesus

(Woman)

Shame on me, immaculate Jesus, for all the wrong I have done. Shame on me for not being a better person. I should not have lied or had bad thoughts. Shame on me, sweet Jesus. Shame on me. I have not been helpful to others and as kind as I could have been. Shame on me, oh great one, Jesus, but oh how I love You so very much. I could have helped the poor, the needy, and sick so much more. I have failed you once again, my precious Jesus. I could have been a better, kinder, sweeter helper to my beloved mom, dad, and brothers. Please forgive me, oh great one up above, loving Jesus. Shame on me. I must work harder helping family, friends, and neighbors, sick and poor. Shame on me for failing You once again, beloved Jesus. Please forgive my many faults. I tried to work so very hard, helping here and there and everywhere. Please give me one more precious chance to live with You in your beloved Heaven and no more shame on me, just endless happiness for everyone and me.

Unbearable

(Man)

Oh, I repeat, do not retreat when your heart skips a beat. It could be the start of a beautiful love affair. So shout with glory, so your new love will appear. You can feel the wonderful music playing in the distance. As it gets louder, your beautiful darling will suddenly appear. You can't believe her overwhelming beauty, her smile, her laughter, you have never seen before. It is definitely one of a kind, a type you will never see again. It holds you in a paralyzing trance, and then you break free, and the words you never heard before flow out of your mouth.

She smiles and laughs from her gorgeous face and says, "Yes, I would like to go with you."

Soon the greatest of love appears, and later we are married with the most precious lives any two persons could ever have.

Mental Cruelty

(Man)

She left me, on that cold winter night, with mental cruelty. She shoved me out the door in subzero weather with just the clothes on my back. I tried to find shelter from that freezing, icy weather. I wandered here and there aimlessly to find shelter and work. How could one woman spew so much terrible mental cruelty? Is there no peace, no kindness in this world of ours? I suffered bitterly day by day with little food and not much shelter.

I saw a woman in trouble. This mangy bum was trying to take her money. I beat him off with savagery, and he turned tail and ran away like a stinky skunk.

She said, "Oh, I am so thankful for your blessed help."

I said, "That dirty bum won't bother you anymore."

I helped her in her truck and she asked, "Can I help you? Do you need work?"

I said, "Oh, yes, ma'am."

So she took me to her ranch and made me foreman of her ranch. We later fell in love and were married. What a great and wonderful life we have now and no more mental cruelty.

Love

(Woman)

I love the way you hug me and the beautiful way you smile and laugh. I want your warm, wet lips, the way they explode when touching mine. It is so wonderful the way you drive me crazy, looking into your beautiful brown eyes and gorgeous face. You are truly a knockout and one of a kind. You paralyze me with unending, precious love. I cannot walk, move, or talk. You have me locked in endless love. Each day our love gets stronger, longer, and sweeter. It swells my heart, which seems to burst in a thousand loves, and then we look, hug, and kiss, and the miracle starts all over again, day after day, year after year. Our love grows stronger until the great One calls us up above where there is an abundance of everlasting love and happiness.

No More Love

(Man)

Why do you treat me so terribly? We were once so much in love, as I still am today. But you must hate me for the way you treat me. I am sure you no longer love me at all. You don't speak to me in kindness anymore. I am so sad. I don't sleep or eat. I pace the floor day and night, hoping you will change your mind. I try to say kind things to you. It seems to go in one ear and out the other. The sweet deeds I do for you are almost instantly forgotten, and my head falls down with overbearing sadness. The tears run down my face like falling rain. I ask you to go with me to a marriage counselor, and you reply with a nasty no. So it's apparent our marriage has failed, and you want no more of me. Then the doorbell rings, and I am served those dreaded divorce papers. So out I go. You have burst the tortured tendons of my heart with your disgusting divorce.

Beloved Mary,
Mother of Precious Jesus

(Woman)

Beloved Mary, Mother of precious Jesus, oh how happy you must have been to have given immaculate birth to your beloved son, our precious Savior Jesus Christ, our God Almighty. It must have made you the happiest mother, knowing your precious, most wonderful Jesus would be our immaculate Savior and religious leader. Everyone will pray to Jesus, adore and respect Him. Oh how proud, grateful, and thankful you must be of your Immortal Son, our Lord and Savior Jesus Christ. Mary, thanks to your beloved help as the precious Mother of Immaculate Jesus, whom we will adore, love, and respect as our one and only Savior and religious leader. Thanks from all of us, one and all, beloved Mary, for immaculate Jesus, for giving us our everything, our precious, religious everything, the great Immaculate Jesus Christ and his beloved Mother Mary.

How Many Men

(Man)

How many men will she go through before she finds number one? I think I might have a chance with her, but will fear hold me back? She looks so beautiful, sexy and sweet, and so smart. I can see why any man would feel such a great honor to go out with her. Men would fight to get a chance to be her date and others to love her. They would pay a fortune. She is certainly in a league of her own, so precious, so pure, certainly one of a kind. That is why it is so easy for her to date any man, for she is a queen among women. Men walk by her, their necks snap around, and their mouths fly open in amazing awe. I have shaken my fear and decide to ask her out, a woman so pure, so immaculate, way out of my league. She says yes. My heart skips a beat. My knees buckle as she so surprises me with that beautiful yes. I must work so hard where many men have failed to land the greatest of ladies to be my wife, my life, existence, and my very being in a land of endless love and happiness. For now and forever, I want her great love.

America

(Woman)

I see the beautiful flag of the United States of America is still blowing over the White House, showing we still have our precious freedom. It still reigns over this beloved U.S.A. where so many soldiers fought for our freedom and to hold us number one, undefeated, and supreme. Many of our precious fighting men died defending this great America as others charged on, defending this beloved U.S.A. we hold, respect, and cherish as the one and only, the greatest. We will and must always defend our beloved America against all enemies who wish to dethrone this beautiful, loving, sacred U.S.A., to always hold it in the highest honor, respect, and supreme love this great America deserves. Thanks to the many beloved soldiers who died defending it and the maimed and living soldiers who fought on so we will always remain number one and undefeated, so our precious freedom will remain now and forever and ever untouched, unchallenged, and unblemished.

Be Careful What You Say

(Woman)

Be careful what you say about me, darling, because I am still madly in love with you. I know we parted on real bad terms, but my love for you continues to grow stronger and stronger. I hope we can get back together again. I will try to call you again to see if, precious, you will go out with me once more, because my love has grown more precious since we parted. I hope you feel the same way about me. Our love before was strong and pure. I can only hope it is again as I dial the phone for a date with you.

I ask you for a date, and your answer back is, (Man) "Yes, I still love you very much."

(Man/Woman) So we fall in love, stronger and more precious, our beautiful second time around.

By Oh, By Oh!

(Man)

My oh, my oh! Where have you gone? By oh, by oh! I miss you so oh, so oh much. Why have you gone by oh, by oh? Every day I search here-E, here-E, but you must be there-E, there-E. You have left me in a tortured mind and tortured body. I cannot give up, for someday I feel you will come back from by oh, by oh and be with me hear-E, here-E. I know I must work day oh, day oh to get you back to me oh, me oh. Everyone keeps asking me where you have gone oh, gone oh, and I said I don't know oh, know oh, but I hope she comes soon oh, soon oh, or my heart will break-E, break-E in millions of piece-E, pieces.

Then in the far off distance I could not believe my eye-E, eyes. I saw her. She was returning to her hubby, hubby. (Man/Woman) so we can have fun-E, fun, and more life-E, life forever and ever and no more bye oh, bye oh, just happy, happy, and love-E, love, for a lifetime of joy-E, joy-E.

Every Day of the Year

(Man)

Every day of the year, I fall in love with you more and more. How could one man love a woman as much as I love you? How could he want to hug, kiss, talk to, and be with you so much? It must happen because you are truly a fantastic, knockout, so precious in every way. We go out, and everyone looks at you with their mouths open in great dismay. How could she even associate with a man like me when she is a woman of outstanding beauty, personality, intelligence, and overwhelming class? So I am sure I must excel with the greatest of love, kindness, and consideration for her to remain with me. It will be so easy for me to reach the highest peaks of love with her because I have never seen a lady with so many outstanding qualities. I will cherish her in so many, many ways, every day of our beloved life.

So Perfect

(Woman)

I know because of your kindness, your sweetness, and your holiness, there had to be a God up above who is so pure and immaculate as our great Savior Jesus Christ, who made you in His image and likeness. Although you are not the great One up above, He has made you one of the finest here on earth. I could never come close to your perfection in any way, but I will do whatever it takes to hold, to cherish, and adore you for all time. I know I must have been so lucky to be chosen and associated with a man so outstanding and perfect as you, my darling sweetheart, my endless love.

A Wink, Wink Here and a Wink, Wink There

(Man)

With a wink, wink here and a wink, wink there, she was so beautiful, sweet and sincere, I could not believe, with a wink, wink here and a wink, wink there. It is so magical that two lives could unite so quickly with a wink, wink here and a wink, wink there. She smiled at me. I smiled at her with a wink, wink here and a wink, wink there. Our love grew so strong day by day, but always such a beautiful wink, wink here and a wink, wink there, and a wonderful lifetime of happiness, love, and kindness with a wink, wink here and a wink, wink there. We have a perfect, loving life. I feel it will go on forever, and we can't believe such a miraculous love blossomed in a greatness so unbelievable as ours with a wink, wink here and a wink, wink there.

My Darling,
the Greatest Lady Singer Ever

(Man)

Sing along with me, my precious darling, make sound so beautiful. It sounds so sweet and wonderful like the beautiful angels singing in the sky. Oh how happy and content it makes me to listen and feel your beautiful music, as it vibrates through all parts of my body. My darling, your very special voice and music, I never heard a more glorious, awesome, loving music enter my eardrums, and that is overwhelmingly demonstrated by the thousands of people at Juilliard, the school of music, rating my beloved sweetheart number one, most outstanding lady singer ever. The audience seemed to cheer, scream for long, long minutes to the greatest, most beloved, and precious lady singer ever. The audience refused to let her leave, yelling more, more, as she sang so very many of her award-winning, number one songs. People yelling, screaming, crying as they couldn't believe the sounds, the beloved music coming from the greatest, most loved lady singer ever—my precious darling, my endless love.

More On and Ons

(Man)

I get up in the morning all happy and joyful, looking for my darling. I see her. I turn it on more and more. She looks back at me, no smile, and turns it off. Why are there so many ons and offs instead of a long and steady flow of ons and ons in place of so many offs and offs? So I will treat my darling so very special, so she will be in the on mode more and more and very few off modes. I can see it is working. She is happy more and more with lots of ons and ons and very little offs. We will keep it that way for a very precious lifetime of endless ons and ons.

I Have the World at My Feet

(Man)

It's the little things you do for me that spin my world out of control. The way you give me clues you love me and I love you day after day. It makes me smile. You are so brilliant. The way you smile and laugh at me makes my heart beat faster and faster with overwhelming love. The little things you do, like touching me, hugging me, and then that special kiss, drive me out of my mind with endless love. We go on a date, you sit by my side, everyone looks at your outstanding beauty, and then they smile at your precious kindness and consideration. I know and feel I am the luckiest man in all the world. We talk and smile and dance along. It makes me feel like a king. It seems to be so very special for you to have fallen in love with me. Oh so wonderful it is, a beautiful woman with your looks, smarts, and everything so outstanding, to have chosen a man like me. I feel I must have gotten help from up above to have landed such a very special lady as you who excels in every way, day after day, year after year.

Come Circle Around Me

(Woman)

Come circle around me. Let the sweet music roar. Oh, how happy I am to hear the beautiful music as it streams in all parts of my body. It makes me feel so great, so complete, and circles around me. Let the fine music play. It makes me feel so great and feel almighty with the wonderful music bouncing off of my heart, mind, and body. So circle around me and let the joyful music play on. The joy fills my heart with everlasting love. I am on a high and addicted to the glory of all the music I adore. It vibrates through my body like an overwhelming symphony. So come, circle around me as the beautiful music plays on. I dance and I rock and sing along with the precious music. I feel so content, so happy. I could do this for hours. It puts me in a world of glory and great and wonderful love for all people. So come circle around me and let that precious music play on, day and night, with no break in sight.

Never Forgotten

(Woman)

I can never forget the beautiful life we once had, the walks on the beach hand in hand, the sweet everlasting kisses and hugs for each other, which melted our hearts together. I am never to forget your precious laugh, your smile, and wonderful personality, but now you are gone up above with a highest priority to help the great one. Oh how you are missed down below by me and everyone else. Oh! So very, very much. It is so terribly hard to see how you are needed elsewhere, but what a special someone so great as you, I know it's truly possible. And Heaven roars with glory and we down below fall down with tears and sadness for the greatest love we have lost.

Shame On Me and You

(Man)

Shame on me for not loving you more and treating you more kindly and sweetly.

(Woman) Shame on me for treating you so very bad, so nasty, and so mean. Once you loved me. Now you hate me. Shame on me.

(Man) Where did I fail you and your precious love? Shame on me. I must not have treated you as the loving wife you once were, to cherish, to treat you so very specially that you deserved shame on me.

(Woman) Why did I not have more patience and love for you and try to get you back to me with love? Shame on me.

(Man) I should have worked day and night to love you more, show you more kindness and consideration you truly deserved. Shame on me.

(Woman) I wish I had treated you with more love and happiness as I did in our early marriage. Shame on me.

(Man/Woman) We both could have been so much better, loving, sweet, kind, and sincere to each other, so we would not have had this terrible divorce and our sadness and remorse. Shame on both of us. We have failed each other and no more happiness, just overwhelming sadness.

Our Precious Daughter June

(Man)

I heard the door screech as it opened in my bedroom. I listened to the gentle smacking on the floor coming closer to me in the brisk morning air. She jumped on my bed and tried to pry my eyes open as she said, (Woman) "Good morning, Daddy. I love you."

(Man) I grabbed and hugged and kissed her and said, "I love you so much, my darling daughter."

Her mom was sleeping and not supposed to be woken because she worked the previous night.

I had the day off, and my daughter, June, said, (Woman) "Where are we going today, Daddy?"

As mommy slept, I said, "Where do you want to go, my darling?"

June said, "Let's go to the park where all the rides are."

(Man) And we had the most beautiful day, ice-cream, cookies, and the greatest of fun, which I have locked in my memory forever to be drawn on time after time.

That little, beautiful, three-foot bundle of precious love is all the world to me and her mommy. We are so very, very thankful for her. She is our everything. She is our life. She is our beautiful world.

Sarah & Meghan,
Our Beautiful Granddaughters

(Man)

Meghan and Sarah, they are all the world to us, Grandma and Grandpa. The evening breeze blew on her gorgeous face that produced a frown, and seconds later, the most beautiful smile. She has stated many times she wants to be an attorney. I know she will be one of the very best. Meghan is her beautiful name to fit her gorgeous face. Meghan is one of two of our beloved granddaughters. The other is also so very pretty and just as gorgeous. Her name is Sarah. She wants to be a teacher of young children and will make a great one. Sarah has great patience to fit her beautiful face and a teaching job. She is working at Costco to help her pay for her schooling, and Meghan is a swimming instructor to help pay for her college.

They are both the apple of me and mommy's eyes. We love them so much. They were such beautiful, gorgeous little granddaughters and now so very pretty and lovely young ladies whose momma and papa, grandpa and grandma think they are the greatest. We will love and help them every year of their very precious lives and hope they find someone equally as wonderful to love and cherish them as we do. They were born to our precious daughter, June.

Happy Birthday, Daughter June

(Man)

Happy birthday, darling June, You are so sweet, so kind. What a precious darling you have been to me and Mama. Your brilliant smile, your wonderful kindnesses, excelled throughout our lifetime. You are loved and held on the highest pedestal by all your family, friends, and neighbors who say everyday what a wonderful daughter you and Trinet have. She is cherished by one and all, and now she has blessed us with two super granddaughters, Sarah and Meghan. They are spitting images in every way of their beloved mother. We could not have wished or prayed for more. They swell our hearts with endless joy. Happy birthday, super-daughter June, and a precious lifetime of many more.